WHERE THE TIDES MEET

ELIJAH HER

F90 PRESS

www.f90press.com

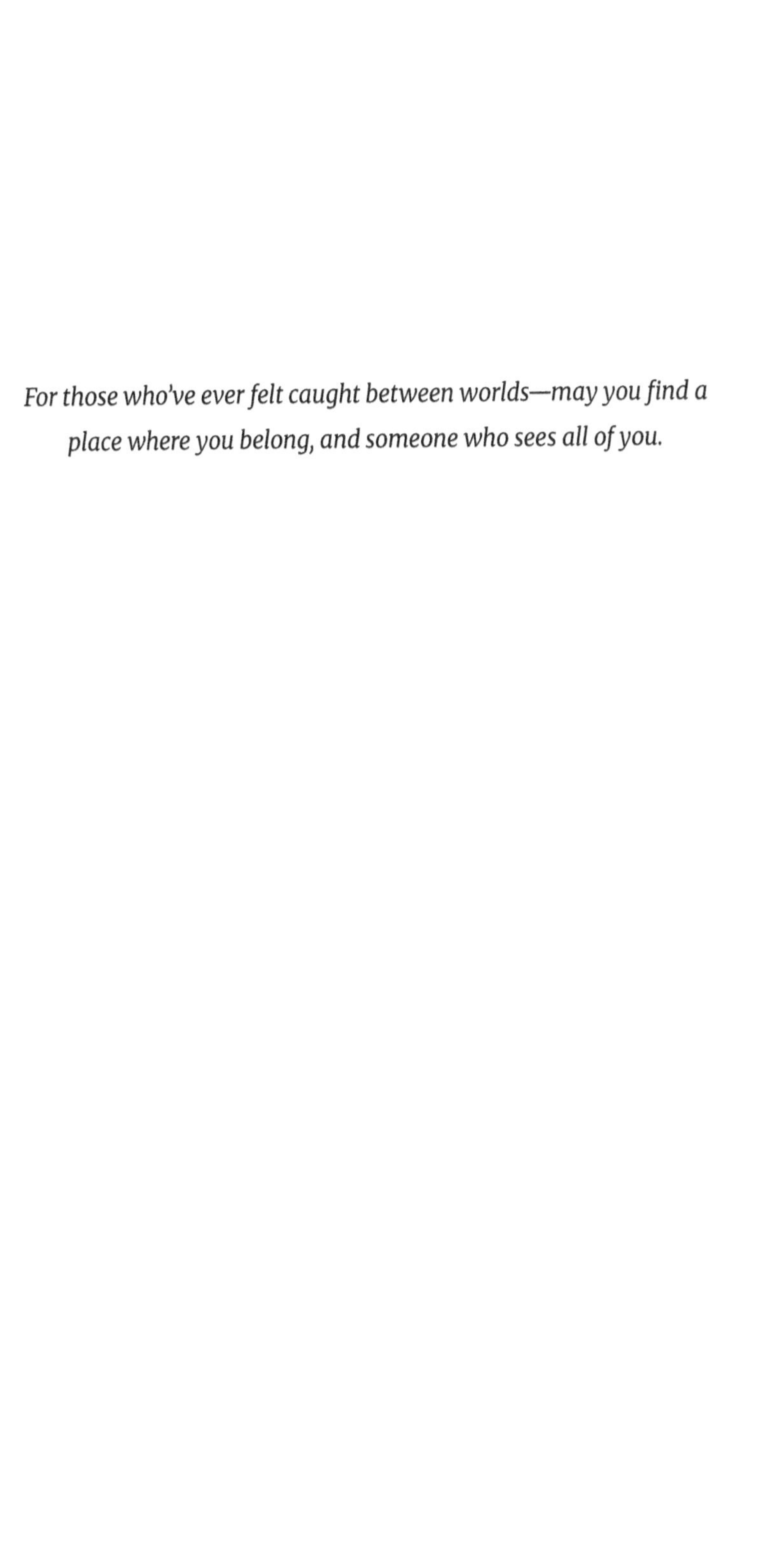

For those who've ever felt caught between worlds—may you find a place where you belong, and someone who sees all of you.

CONTENT NOTES

Where the Tides Meet includes explicit sexual content. It also touches on themes some may be sensitive to or find triggering:

Depictions of physical violence, and murder. Societal and familial pressures. External homophobia.

PRONUNCIATION GUIDE

Aeronith *(AIR-uh-nith)*
Balthvidae *(BALTH-vee-day)*
Beaumir *(BOH-meer)*
Brisa *(BREE-suh)*
Coralie *(KOR-uh-lee)*
Elisienne *(eh-lee-SYDEN)*
Evren *(Ev-ren)*
Harlowe *(HAR-loh)*
Isolde *(ee-ZOLD)*
Lopharius *(lo-FAIR-ee-us)*
Mathis de Clairvaux *(MAH-tees duh clair-VOH)*
Marella *(meh-RELL-uh)*
Morvena *(mor-VEEN-uh)*
Nerielle *(NEH-ree-uhl)*
Nerina *(neh-REE-nuh)*
Nerídes *(neh-REE-deez)*
Olivier Fenais *(oh-lee-VEER fun-NAY)*
Roland LeVesque *(ROH-lund luh-VESK)*
Rylen *(RYE-len)*
Seraphina *(seh-ruh-FEE-nuh)*
Titus *(TY-tus)*
Valtherion *(val-THAIR-ee-on)*

Chapter One

Seawitch. That was what they called her. A heretic. A traitor. A creature who had defied the sacred order of the deep, who had tasted the air above and let it change her. They whispered of her cruelty, of the unnatural magic that clung to her like the brine of the shallows. But I knew better.

She was the only one who saw what needed to be done.

The waters around me thickened, pressing against my skin like a great, unseen hand, urging me to turn back. The light from above had long since dissolved into darkness, leaving only the pale, pulsing glow of my lanternfish companion to guide me. Its bioluminescence trembled against jagged walls of black stone, shadows stretching and shifting as I descended further into the abyss. The current here was sluggish, oppressive, thick with the kind of silence that swallowed sound whole.

I spoke her name anyway.

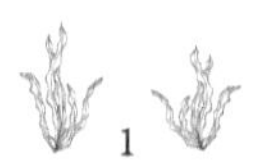

"Morvena."

The word drifted into the dark, fragile as a dying ember. My voice did not echo—it was devoured, lost to the crushing pressure of the depths. The cold gnawed at my flesh, sharper with every beat of my tail. My pulse quickened, not merely from the weight of the ocean pressing in on me, but from the weight of something far heavier.

Desperation.

The humans had gone too far. For as long as I had drawn breath, they had sought to ruin us—to poison our waters, to strip our seas bare with their nets and hooks and hunger. We had always hidden in the depths, watching as they grew bolder, as their greed carved deeper wounds into our world. But today... today, we struck back. *I struck back.*

My grip tightened on the sodden fabric trailing beside me, its dark weave billowing with each movement. Blood had dyed the waters red, mingling like ink spilled upon a parchment. I had commanded the sea to rise, and she had answered, crushing and dragging them down into the abyss where they did not belong.

And yet, even now, the weight of it pressed against my ribs, unfamiliar and unrelenting.

I had never been so close to them before, not like this. Not since I was a minnow, when I had first glimpsed a human boy on the shore. He had been small, soft, his eyes wide with wonder rather than fear. There had been no cruelty in him, no hunger for conquest—only admiration, only awe.

What had changed?

Perhaps they had all been soft things once. Perhaps, like the sea itself, they had only learned to be merciless when the world demanded it of them.

Just as I had.

The arches of the sea witch's palace loomed ahead, shrouded in veils of luminescent algae. Their eerie, greenish glow clung to the coral spires and weathered stone columns, casting spectral light through the shifting waters. Between them, shadows curled and twisted, their murmurs threading through the silence like a hymn I dared not heed.

I hovered at the threshold—a great archway carved with symbols I could not read, yet felt thrumming in my bones. Power lived here. Not the call of the tides, not the steady pull of the sea's embrace, but something foreign. Something I had been raised to fear.

It was not the ocean that answered Morvena's command.

I had heard whispers of human magic, of the chaos it wove, its nature not of current and flow but of force—raw, unyielding, corrupting. It was not born of the sea but of something older, something untethered.

"Morvena!" My voice broke, carried away by the restless tide. "I... I need you. Please, hear me."

The water shuddered. A pulse of energy rippled outward, unseen but unmistakable, and the cold that clung to me sharpened into something crueler, more biting. I swallowed against the instinct to flee, my hands curling into fists at my sides.

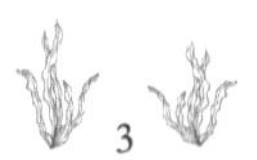

From the depths, she emerged.

Morvena moved as if she were one with the water, her form unfurling from the darkness in languid, inescapable grace. Her hair spilled in inky tendrils around her, a living mass that coiled and shifted as though it breathed. Her eyes—luminous as the ethereal bloom of a mauve stinger—caught the ghostly light and held it, made it her own.

Even in exile, she bore the presence of royalty. Not in name, nor in title anymore, but in the quiet, undeniable weight of power.

"You are brave to come here, Prince," she said, her voice smooth, yet heavy with the undertow of something vast and unrelenting. "Or foolish. What would your father think of you visiting me, cousin?"

The title coiled through me like a serpent, its familiarity laced with mockery.

I bowed my head, my throat tight. "My people—our people—are dying," I said, the words raw, torn from some place deep within. "Father refuses to act. He thinks to do so would incite war." A pause, a breath, then I met her gaze once more, letting the conviction settle into my voice. "But we are already at war."

She tilted her head, studying me with an unreadable expression. Not warm. Not cruel. A silent current pulling in both directions. Her amethyst gaze flicked to the scrap of fabric I held—the torn remnants of a human ship.

4

"What makes you think I can help you?" she murmured. "I am bound here, forbidden from calling upon the sea."

I lifted my chin. "But you do not call upon the sea," I countered. "You call upon the chaos—like the humans do. Does their power not reach even these depths?" My grip tightened around the fabric. "I need you to show me how to wield it. I need to do something. If I can stop the humans from taking more lives, from desecrating our waters... I will convince my father to pardon you. I can show that your power can be used for good."

Silence fell between us, thick as silt, the weight of it pressing against my ribs.

Then Morvena laughed. Low, languid. A sound that did not rise so much as curl through the water, dark and knowing. "And you think I have the power to help you with that?" she purred.

Silence stretched between us, thick as the depths themselves.

Perhaps this was a mistake. What could one merfolk do alone? Without my father's backing, without our armies, without the weight of a crown behind my words? My grip slackened, fingers unfurling around the scrap of fabric, though I did not yet release it. Even now, it felt like an anchor, a tether to the conviction that had driven me here.

"Even if I had the means to grant you the power you seek, Prince Rylen, what would you do with it?" she mused. "Would you drag the humans into the abyss, drown them in the

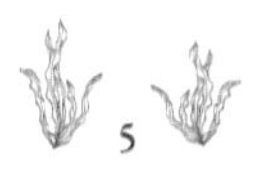

very waters they dare to trespass? Would you stain the sea red until even the tides rejected your name?" A slow smile curled her lips. "Human blood is a filthy thing, you know. It lingers." Her voice turned almost sweet. "King Aeronith would sooner cast you from his sight than see you return tainted by their magic. He would call you a monster. And perhaps he would be right."

My throat tightened. *I had already committed those crimes.* The sea and my soul were stained with human blood because of my own actions. I was already a monster—but what is a monster, if their sins were born not of cruelty, but devotion? If the hands that killed did so in the name of others, not themselves?

"Then... then what should I do?" The words tasted of salt and surrender, though I willed them to hold firm. "They take our people. Drag them to the surface. We never see them again. I don't—I can't—" I forced a breath, steadying myself. "We cannot remain idle."

Her gaze darkened, something unreadable flickering in the abyss of her pupils. She moved, slow and deliberate, her tail flicking lazily as she circled me. The shifting glow of the lanternfish illuminated her in fragments—scales of iridescent violet and obsidian, dark tendrils of hair curling in the current, lips parted in something that was not quite a smile.

"I cannot give you access to the magic you seek," she murmured, "but I can offer you something else." Her gaze sharpened, the weight of it pressing against my skin. "But everything comes at a price, my dear. Are you willing to pay it?"

"Yes." The word escaped me in a breath.

Morvena's fingers traced the curve of my jaw, tilting my chin upward. She was close now, so close I could see the delicate webbing between her fingers, the faint shimmer of scales dusting her wrists and cheekbones.

"Are you sure?"

I held her gaze, my pulse a steady drumbeat in my ears.

"I would do anything for my people."

Her smile deepened.

"Good."

In one swift motion, she plucked the fabric from my grasp, inspecting it with a strange sort of reverence. Then, without another word, she turned, slipping through the great archway beyond.

I hesitated only a moment before following.

The lanternfish cast our shadows against the walls as we descended deeper into Morvena's domain. The water here felt heavier, thick with unseen currents, charged with something ancient. Pillars of dark stone loomed around us, their surfaces slick with bioluminescent moss, casting eerie halos of green and gold. The floor was littered with the remnants of the past—tarnished mirrors reflecting distorted images, shattered glass orbs that once held substance, the bones of creatures that had long since succumbed to the abyss.

At the heart of the chamber, a throne carved from black coral rose like a monolith, its twisted spires reaching upward as if yearning for a surface it would never touch.

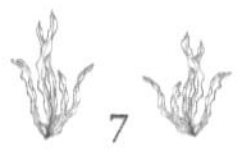

Morvena settled against it with effortless grace. "Now," she purred, running a delicate claw over the torn fabric in her hands, "let us see what the humans have left us."

Her fingers glided over the fabric, her touch slow, almost indulgent, as if it were something sacred. The dark cloth lay draped across the iridescent sweep of her tail, gold-threaded embroidery catching the dim, flickering light in the abyss.

"It seems," she mused, "that the humans who dare trespass these waters are not mere sailors or merchants. They are nobility." She loosened her grip, and the fabric began its slow descent, unraveling like spilled ink into the deep.

I lunged, fingers curling around the cloth, pulse quickening as I turned it over, tracing the intricate sigil woven into its surface—foreign symbols, imagery beyond my understanding.

"That," she continued, watching me with quiet amusement, "is the crest of Gadimore, a kingdom of men that lay just beyond the shores of Aserian."

"A kingdom?" I echoed.

Morvena's lips curved. "Just as we rule beneath the waves, they rule above them. The human world is not one, but many—divided by power, by land, by greed. Find their king, their ruler, and you will find the hand that orchestrates these attacks. Kill him, make him bow, I do not care."

I clenched the fabric tighter. "And how am I to find him? I cannot walk among men."

A slow, knowing smile.

"That is the gift I can give you."

The water between us stirred, charged with unseen force.

"Once the magic of chaos is within one," she whispered, "it does not matter how deep you are—it will always answer your call. But chaos magic is of the land, of the sky. I cannot teach you its ways while you remain in the tide's embrace. But I can bestow its gifts upon you. I can grant you the means to walk among men."

The words wrapped around me like a net, tightening with every breath. To walk upon the land, to feel the air of the surface on my skin—it would mark me, taint me, as it had tainted her. And yet... if I returned a hero, would that not wash the stain away? Would my father not welcome me back with pride, rather than condemnation?

I swallowed hard. "What is the price?"

"It is very simple," she said softly. "There is a man. A prince."

A pause. A flicker of something unreadable in her gaze. "His eyes," she murmured, "are green as the emerald grottos. His hair, dark as the ship you sent to ruin." She tilted her head. "Bring me his heart."

A chill rippled through me. "His heart?"

She hummed, her tail flicking lazily. "Chaos is not limitless, dear cousin. It must be taken to be used." She sank lower, her fingers sifting through the sand, lifting it in a loose fist. "To wield chaos, one must expand it." Slowly, she let the grains fall, a cascade of glimmering specks swallowed by the dark. "And once chaos is spent, there is none left to call upon."

She dusted off her hands, glancing up at me through her lashes. "Helping you will require much of my power. You wouldn't want me defenseless down here, stripped of both sea and chaos, would you?"

A smile—slow, knowing.

"It is a simple trade," she purred. "Chaos for chaos. His heart is tainted with it. That is the price."

Take another human life. Possibly an innocent life.

One life, against the hundreds of ours they had stolen. There were no innocents. It would be nothing to take his life, just balance.

Morvena watched me, patient as the tide.

"Well, Rylen?" Her voice was a whisper, a strand of seafoam drifting through the water. "Do we have a deal? Walk among men for a prince's heart?"

A merfolk's word was not a trifling thing. A promise uttered, a vow sworn, a deal made—it wove itself into the currents, bound by salt and tide, carried on the breath of the waves. The sea did not forget, nor did it forgive those who failed to honor their oaths. A debt sworn beneath its gaze was a debt that must be paid, whether in flesh or in fate.

I exhaled, slow and steady, forcing my voice into something unyielding.

"Yes."

She did not say another word, only let her lips curve into an unnerving smile, her tail flicking idly through the water. Her fingers drifted through the debris scattered along the seabed, moving with the care of a predator indulging in play.

Fragments of broken glass—sharp-edged and glinting like the teeth of deep-sea beasts—shifting.

"I have basked in the sun before," she murmured, voice lilting like a song half-forgotten. "Breathed the air of men, lingered on their shorelines." Her fingers closed around a shard of glass—pale blue like a drowned man's lips. "I was curious once, foolish in my youth. I lingered too long, listened too closely." Her grip tightened, the water stirring with the force of it. "That was how I found chaos. Or rather, how it found me."

She lifted the shard, and I felt the shift in the current, something imperceptible yet undeniable. The glass trembled, its edges smoothing, its surface weathered by unseen hands. Twine wove itself around its sides, curling like seaweed caught in a tide, until it was no longer a discarded fragment, but something shaped—fashioned into a talisman.

Morvena held it out, the makeshift necklace swaying between her fingers.

"Slip this around your neck," she said, "and you will be as they are. You will walk among humans. But beware, cousin—should you lose it, the form will break, and the sea will reclaim you."

She watched as I turned the talisman over in my palm, my thumb running along the smooth surface.

"The magic within it is not endless," she said, voice a whisper against the currents. "Every step you take upon the land, every breath of their air, will drain it. Once it loses all its chaos, its shape will return to what it once was—sharp, jagged.

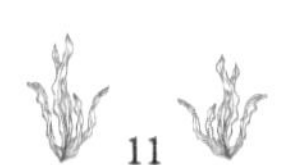

And you…" Her lips curved, slow and cruel. "You will remain as you should be. Merfolk."

I swallowed, my fingers tightening around the talisman. The weight of it suddenly felt heavier, as if I were holding a blade rather than a trinket.

"The human world is filled with wonders and horrors alike," Morvena continued, her gaze dark with warning. "Tread carefully, and do not let them know what you are. Find Gadimore. Ruin their kingdom. And bring me my heart."

I met her eyes, a silent promise passing between us as I bowed my head.

"Thank you, Morvena."

"Ah, but one last thing, dear Rylen."

She moved closer, the water thick with her presence. A single finger traced my chest, slow and deliberate, until her nail pressed just over my heart.

"We agreed upon a prince's heart," she said, her smile sharp enough to cut. "If you fail me, if you bring me anything less than the one I seek…" A light pressure, a silent threat. "I will take yours instead."

The weight of her words settled against my ribs, colder than the deepest trench.

"I understand." I murmured, my throat tight. "I will not fail."

Satisfied, she drifted back into the shadows of her throne, her eyes gleaming with something unreadable.

I did not linger. With a flick of my tail, I turned, leaving the abyss behind, rising toward the lighter waters above. The

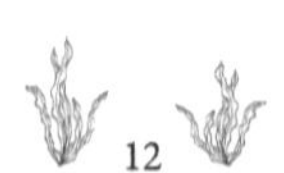

chill of Morvena's domain faded, replaced by the familiar warmth of home—yet even as I swam, I could not shake the feeling that something of her lingered still, curling in the depths of my soul like an unseen current, waiting.

I should have turned back. Returned to the palace, to my father's cold stare and my mother's quiet sorrow. To my siblings, to my people—to the ones who would call me reckless, who would call me mad. They would try to stop me. They would say I had condemned myself the moment I sought out the seawitch.

Perhaps they were right.

But the humans would not stop. Their ships would come, as they always had, casting their shadows over our waters, their nets swallowing us whole. They would take and take, leaving only wreckage and blood in their wake. And we would remain below, watching, waiting, drowning in our own silence.

No longer.

I tightened my grip on the fabric, the royal insignia of a kingdom I had never seen but already despised. *Gadimore.* That was its name. The name of the rot at the heart of the surface world. The name of the kingdom that would fall.

I surged forward, my tail cutting through the dark waters, following the shimmer of the moon above. The sea, my sea, stretched endless before me. But beyond it—beyond the waves and the foam—was the shore.

And I was going to cross it.

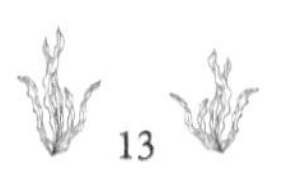

Chapter Two

I focused on the sea, on the rhythmic crash of waves against the shore. The tide was low, retreating, as if the ocean itself wished to pull me back into its depths. The sea was louder up here. Wilder. A voice in the wind, in the current, whispering to me, pleading. *Turn back.* My fingers sifted through the wet sand, lifting a handful only to let it slip through my grasp, each grain a fleeting thing, vanishing before I could hold it for long.

The moonlight stretched across the water, silver on black, an unbroken shimmer that led to the horizon. And yet, my gaze returned to the shore—to where I sat, half-submerged, the tide curling gently around me, as if testing whether I still belonged to it.

My fingers traced the talisman resting against my palm, the cool glass catching the moon's reflection. Blue, pale and luminous, like the scales of my tail. Had Morvena chosen this color with purpose? A reminder of all I was leaving behind?

A taunt, perhaps, or a cruel kind of encouragement. A tether to my home. A warning not to forget.

A voice broke the stillness. Soft, curious. Yet even in its gentleness, it startled me.

"What are you doing?"

I exhaled sharply, curling my fingers around the talisman, hiding its glow within my palm.

"Coralie." Her name left my lips in a breath, low, wary. I turned, meeting her gaze. "How did you find me?"

She swam closer, her form cutting lightly through the water's surface, dark ruby locks floating around her like trailing ribbons of seaweed.

"The sea talks, remember?" Coralie's lips curved, the warmth of her smile not quite enough to thaw the cold coil of resolve in my chest. Her eyes, wide and speckled brown, studied me as if she could decipher my thoughts simply by looking long enough.

The lanternfish must have told her where to find me. I sighed internally.

"I was searching for you," she continued, voice gentle yet insistent. "King Aeronith and Queen Nerielle plan to commence the Drift when the moon is at its highest. You are to attend, Your Highness."

The Drift. The ceremony for the dead.

I clenched my jaw, forcing my gaze to remain on the horizon rather than meet hers. I knew my duty. Knew what was expected. But how many more times must I watch the sea take the remains of my people? The Drifts had become more

frequent, the humans growing bolder, venturing beyond their shores, beyond their netted cages and fishing lines, thirsting for more than just what land provides.

When they learned of us centuries ago, it had been fear at first—on both sides. We had tried for peace. Tried to stay away. But they always returned, their ships laden with iron and steel, with hooks and nets meant to drag us gasping from our waters.

What they did with the merfolk they took, we did not know. But I intended to find out.

"We have been friends since we were minnows," I murmured. "Such formalities are unnecessary."

"I know." A teasing lilt touched her voice. "But they bother you, so I like them."

She laughed softly, the sound at odds with the weight pressing against my ribs. Then, with a flick of her tail, she began to drift backward, her scales catching the moonlight in shades of dark red and white. "Come," she urged, gesturing toward the open water. "Before whispers spread that we are this close to the humans."

"I am not attending the Drift."

Coralie stilled. The playfulness in her expression dimmed, replaced by something heavier, something I had seen before in her eyes when she feared for me.

"Your mother and father will be displeased," she said at last, not as a reprimand, but a reminder. A warning. She had always been the one to steady me, the one to bring me back when I strayed too far from the sea's pull. Perhaps that was why

my parents adored her, why they spoke of her as though she were the tether that might keep me from drifting into ruin.

But they forgot that friendships go both ways.

And I was not always the best influence on her.

"They killed another of ours," I said, voice tight. "I have to stop this."

"With all the power of the sea at Aeronith's command, even he cannot keep the humans from our waters. What makes you think you can, Rylen?"

"Because I spoke to Morvena."

Her eyes widened. A sharp inhale, a flicker of fear.

"Rylen," she whispered. And then she was beside me, pressing up against the shoreline, one hand braced against the sand, the other cupping my cheek as if she could ground me, hold me in place before I slipped too far. "I know you are grieving. I know you are angry. But the seawitch? Are you mad? You cannot listen to her."

Her gaze dropped from mine, sweeping past the sand and up toward the shore, toward the dark stretch of trees, the rising silhouette of human structures built from stone and light.

"What did you do?" Her voice was hushed, fearful. Then, before I could answer, she reached for me, her fingers grazing the gills along my neck, sending a shiver down my spine. "You must not stay like this for long. Do you feel it? The air is unnatural—it will change you. Perhaps it already has." She took my hand, pulling gently. "Come. You are not well." she pleaded. "Let the sea clear your thoughts."

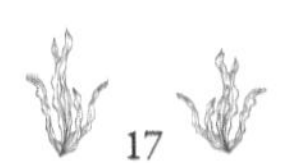

I hesitated.

Then, I pulled away.

"Rylen, do you wish to be condemned to the darkness like Morvena?" Coralie's voice wavered, threading concern between each syllable. "It is lightless, endless—a pit where even our eyes cannot see. It is cold, and the creatures—"

"I know." The words cut from me, sharper than I intended.

She flinched, her gaze dropping to the sea, to the silver foam curling at the shore. "You are my best friend. My prince. My future king." A pause, then softer, "I do not wish to lose you."

Her plea struck something deep within me.

"I'm sorry." The words barely left my lips, more breath than sound.

"This is truly what you wish to do?"

"Yes."

She exhaled, a slow and knowing breath. "Then I will not stop you." A small, fragile smile ghosted across her lips, but it did not reach her eyes. "Not that I think I could, even if I tried."

We, the merfolk, were creatures of longing. There was always something that called to us—a lure as inevitable as the tide. Sometimes it was an object, gleaming and forgotten beneath the waves. Sometimes a soul, a voice that threaded itself through our very being. Sometimes, merely an idea, a notion that burrowed deep and refused to let go.

For some, that call led to madness. For others, obsession. And for too many, it became their undoing. I knew that was what she feared in me.

"Coralie." I reached for her, guiding her hand to my tail, palm up. Then, slowly, my fingers trailed up, curling around the intricate silver cuff on my bicep—the symbol of my lineage, the mark of a prince of the sea. With careful reverence, I removed it, pressing it into her palm.

"Keep this for me," I murmured. "Keep it safe until I return."

She clutched it tightly. "I will."

I pulled her into an embrace, arms wrapped tightly around her, anchoring myself in her warmth for just a moment longer. My fingers curled around the hidden talisman, the cool weight of it pressing into my palm.

Coralie let out a long breath, her form melting against mine. "Mind yourself," she whispered. "Do not let them take you... do not let them change you."

"I won't."

I refused to be remade in their image—twisted into something that was no longer my own. And if they took me, I would take many of them down with me.

She pulled away first, her hands lingering for only a moment before she turned, diving into the sea. Her body cut through the water, disappearing beneath the surface, fading into the darkness beyond the shallows.

And then I was alone.

This was it.

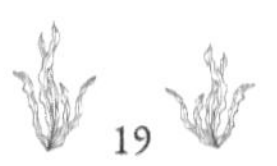

I lifted the talisman, and slipped the twine over my head, pressing the charm to my chest.

For a breath, there was nothing.

Then agony.

A searing, damning warmth, as if my very essence was being unraveled thread by thread. I collapsed onto the sand, spine bowing, fingers clawing at my throat. My gills—my lifeline—began to knit shut, the delicate slits sealing over as though they had never been there at all. I choked, heaving against the sudden, suffocating stillness, lungs burning for something they had never needed to take.

And then—I inhaled.

Air. Crisp and sharp. It filled me, spread through me, foreign and wrong and yet—sustaining. I gasped, rolling onto my stomach as the pain coiled down my spine, burning through muscle, through bone. My tail—

A sharp, tearing sensation ripped through me, my vision going white with the sheer force of it. My forehead pressed against the damp sand, fingers digging into the earth as my body convulsed. My tail—it was breaking, splitting apart, shifting. Bone reformed, muscle stretched and twisted into something unfamiliar.

And then—stillness.

I pushed myself upright, trembling, the effort sending sharp tremors through my limbs. My body wracked with exhaustion, cold and weak as though I had swum from ocean to ocean without rest. Steady hands sank into the wet sand, anchoring me as the tide swept over my form, cool and

indifferent to my suffering. I shifted, instinctively expecting the familiar weight of my tail, the smooth ease of movement that had guided me through the sea since birth. But there was nothing—nothing but the strange, disjointed weight of my own body, reshaped into something unnatural. Something human.

I glanced down.

Two pale appendages stretched from my torso, foreign and fragile, the flesh mottled where the waves lapped against them. Limbs, split where there should have been a single, powerful fin. The joints bent awkwardly as I struggled to adjust, my breath catching at the sheer wrongness of it. When I tried to move, a sharp discomfort flared where the sand scraped against my newly formed skin—so exposed, so vulnerable.

A flicker of unease curled in my chest, deepening into something darker when my gaze traveled between the stumps. My stomach clenched.

I had never seen a human without their garments. I had never considered, never known—

I averted my eyes, heat flashing through me as realization settled like a stone in my gut. How absurd, how reckless that humans carried their weaknesses so openly, their vulnerability laid bare for all to see. It was a wonder they survived at all, with their delicate skin and exposed reproduction organs, with their endless need to multiply like rabbitfish to make up for their fragility.

And why did it look like that? Smaller than I imagined—singular, lesser perhaps—but there was something else as well, something foreign that clung beneath it. A second

shape, unfamiliar and soft. I couldn't decide if I mourned the difference or marveled at it.

A sharp gust of wind rolled in from the shore, curling around my newly formed body, and I shivered violently. The cold bit at me in ways it never had before, pressing against my damp skin, burrowing deep into my bones. A new, human sensation—one I despised already.

Cursing under my breath, I seized the torn remnants of black cloth beside me, wrapping it around my waist with stiff, uncertain fingers. The rough fabric chafed against my too-sensitive skin, but it was better than the alternative.

Better than this shameful exposure.

I exhaled, slow and measured, and forced my hands to still. This was merely another transformation, another trial to endure. It was temporary. It had to be.

Gadimore would fall, and I would return to the sea.

I rolled onto my side, bracing my arms against the shifting sands. The moment I tried to rise, my new limbs buckled, sending me collapsing back into the embrace of the sand. Frustration curled through me.

"Tides," I muttered, voice low, seething.

I had watched humans before—from the secrecy of the waves, from the shadows beneath their ships. I had seen how they moved, how they balanced upon these double-tailed stumps. It did not seem so difficult. If any mer could master this, it would be me.

I gathered myself once more, pressing my palms into the damp earth, forcing my weight onto these unfamiliar limbs.

They trembled beneath me, but I remained upright, unyielding. The stone and forest loomed ahead, dark and dense, a narrow path winding up toward the land beyond. That was where I needed to go—to the humans.

I lifted one limb, mirroring the careful, deliberate steps I had observed from afar. The instant my foot touched the ground, my balance wavered. A moment later, I was falling, the world tilting as I crashed onto the shore with a dull thud. The sand swallowed me whole, the tide curling over my form as if in quiet mockery.

A growl built in my throat.

Again, I forced myself up. Slower this time. Calculated. One limb forward, then the other, bent slightly at the joint—yes, that made it easier. The effort sent a tremor through my body, muscles burning with strain, but I persisted, inching my way toward the treeline.

My fingers found purchase against the low-hanging branches, gripping them as I pulled myself further inland. The earth beneath me shifted from sand to dirt, and then to something else—rough, unyielding stone. A path.

The palms of my stumps pressed against its coarse surface as I followed the winding way. Ahead, rising in the distance, were the towering structures of human civilization. I only needed to reach their city. To stand before their king and make him see reason. To demand he keep his people from our waters, that he return the merfolk they had stolen. And if he refused... well, then I would kill him.

Simple.

The ground beneath me trembled suddenly, a rhythmic clanking echoing through the night. I turned sharply—too sharply. My unsteady limbs betrayed me, and I tumbled backward onto the unforgiving stone. A shadow loomed over me, vast and thundering, a beast of immense size dragging a wooden vessel in its wake.

I barely had time to brace myself.

"Easy, easy now!"

The gruff voice came from behind the creature, and in an instant, it slowed, halting just before it would have crushed me beneath its heavy hooves. The great black snout huffed a gust of warm air against my face, and I stilled, uncertain whether it was a gesture of irritation or curiosity. The beasts of the sea, I understood—they spoke without words, their movements and language fluid as the currents that carried them. But this creature was unfamiliar, its dark, glassy eyes revealing nothing of its thoughts.

"Have you taken harm?"

The voice belonged to a human—an older man, small beside the beast, his face lined with age, his hair and beard streaked in white and gray. He regarded me with concern, his hand resting upon the creature's mane.

"You are fortunate," he continued. "A moment later, and she might have trampled you." His fingers ran through the animal's coarse hair. "A death by trampling beneath a horse's hooves is a fate I would wish upon no man."

"Horse," I murmured, tasting the unfamiliar word as I tried to stand, my limbs wobbling

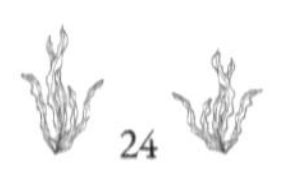

He frowned. "Have you taken a blow to the head? What ails your legs?" He took a step closer, brows knitting as he studied my unsteady form.

I tried to move back, but my limbs wavered beneath me.

"Legs?"

"Yes, your legs. Your feet." His arm came around me, steadying me before I could collapse again. "You reek of salt and brine... And where are your clothes?"

I stared at him.

Did all humans speak so much?

"Come, let me take you into the village. You may stay with me for the night—it is only myself now, so you would not be imposing," he said, guiding me toward the wooden vessel hitched behind his beast. A carriage, he explained, its frame worn with age but sturdy still. The horse shifted, its breath clouding in the cool night air, great dark eyes turning toward me with unreadable intent.

The man shed a layer of his clothing—humans wore so many, draped in fabric as though their bodies alone could not withstand the elements. Still, I took the offered garment, clutching it close as warmth bled back into my skin.

"You have my thanks," I murmured.

It was strange, this kindness. I had not thought humans capable of it. But then, he did not know what I was. His mercy would sour, I was sure, if he learned the truth.

"Olivier Fenais," he offered as his hands found the leather straps, urging the beast forward with a practiced ease.

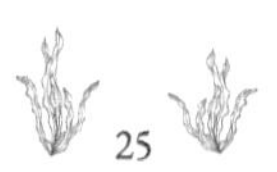

I hesitated before speaking. "Rylen."

"You are not from Harlowe, are you?" Olivier cast me a sidelong glance. "We are a modest fishing port, and we know our own. I would remember a face such as yours."

"Harlowe?" I echoed. "Is that not Gadimore?" I gestured toward the road ahead, the land stretching vast and unfamiliar before me.

"All of this is the Kingdom of Gadimore," he said simply.

"Where... where would I find its king and queen?"

"Them?" He gave a quiet chuckle. "You'll find the king in the capital, at the royal palace. A fair distance from here."

I fell silent, turning the thought over in my mind. The realms of men were more fragmented than I had imagined. Morvena had spoken of their lands being divided, but I had not realized their kingdoms were, too. Still, I doubted their reach could rival that of the sea. Beneath the waves, all waters belonged to my father, the entire reach of the Aserian Sea bending to his rule. North, south, east, and west—it was all one kingdom.

"Have you business with the crown?" Olivier asked.

"Yes," I answered slowly. "I bear a message for them." A half-truth, slipping from my tongue with practiced ease.

"Then let us worry about that come morning," he said. "Tonight, we'll see you fed, clothed, and rested."

There were echoes of familiarity in the human settlement, an uncanny reflection of the world I had left behind. Their dwellings, though rigid and earthbound, held an order not unlike the sprawling coral citadels of my own kind. But

where we carved our homes from the bones of the sea, theirs were built from stone and felled wood, thatched with golden reeds that rustled in the wind.

Olivier was kind. Patient. And yet, no matter how warmly he spoke, I could not shake the feeling of being an imposition. He reassured me time and time again that it was no trouble, but I saw the quiet questions in his eyes, the careful way he studied me when I failed to understand the simplest of things. A man who had lived among his own kind all his life should not need to be taught how to walk, what a door and chair was. He did not press me, too polite to pry, yet his curiosity hung in the air between us, unspoken but ever-present.

"I've set a place for you in my son's old room," he said, setting something in front of me on the wooden table. "There are clothes there for you as well—nothing extravagant, but they should fit."

I nodded, but my attention had already drifted to what sat before me. A bowl, filled with something that steamed and swirled in rich, earthen colors. "It's stew," Olivier explained, watching me. "Just vegetables. Nothing fancy, but it should do the trick."

A strange sensation stirred in my stomach—hunger, I realized, though it felt different on land, heavier, sharper. I had never smelled food before. There was no scent beneath the waves, only the shifting of currents, the electric pulse of life moving through the deep. Even when I had surfaced, all I had

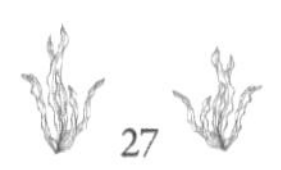

ever known was the salt of the sea. But this—this was warm, spiced, layered with something impossibly rich.

I stared down at it, uncertain.

"Well, staring at it won't fill that stomach of yours," Olivier chuckled, setting a wooden object beside me. "Here. A spoon."

I picked it up hesitantly, feeling its smooth, worn surface between my fingers.

"You hold the bowl like this," he demonstrated, lifting his own, "then scoop the stew with the spoon and bring it to your mouth. Chew, swallow. Try not to choke—I don't need you dying in here."

I did as he instructed, bringing the first spoonful to my lips. The heat startled me. It pressed against my tongue, unfamiliar and heavy, a burst of sensation unlike anything I had ever known. Salt, but not the salt of the sea—deeper, more complex, mingling with something earthy, something sweet. I hesitated, then let it pass my tongue, swallowing carefully. The warmth spread down my throat, unfurling in my chest, soothing the raw ache in my stomach.

I had never eaten like this before. In the sea, we absorbed what we needed from the water, from the life that pulsed around us. This act—this deliberate consumption—felt almost invasive, as if I were taking something that did not belong to me. And yet, it filled me, in a way I had not realized I could be filled.

Olivier smiled, satisfied. "Not so bad, is it?"

I shook my head, still lost in the lingering taste, the warmth settling in my bones.

No, not so bad at all.

"You spoke of a son," I said, my voice quiet, careful.

Olivier nodded, stirring embers in the hearth before sitting once more. "Jonah. He serves in the King's Fleet, stationed in the capital." He paused, as if weighing his next words. "The Coastal Guard," he clarified, reading the furrow in my brow. "The King's men who keep our shores safe—from pirates, from invading fleets."

The stew in my bowl cooled, untouched. The weight of his words pressed against my ribs, an unseen tide pulling at the fragile ground beneath me. His son was one of them—one of the humans who trespassed upon our waters, who turned our kingdom into a hunting ground. My fingers curled over the fraying fabric wrapped around my waist.

Olivier's gaze drifted to it as well. His voice, though gentle, held the sharp edge of curiosity. "That cloth—it's from the sail of a Fleet vessel, is it not?" A pause. "Are you a Coastal Guard?"

I did not answer.

If my silence disappointed him, he did not let it show. "Mm," he murmured, retreating from the subject with quiet grace. "Well, you are safe now. I'll draw a bath for you, and then you should rest. Tomorrow, we'll see to getting you to the capital."

He stood, crossing the small room with the unhurried movements of a man who had long grown accustomed to

solitude. The firelight caught in the silver strands of his hair as he filled a pail with water. I watched, wordless, as he carried bucket after bucket into the adjoining room, the sound of water sloshing against wood filling the quiet.

And yet, my thoughts wandered. How could a man so patient, so unfaltering in his kindness, have fathered a son who pledged his life to invasion? To conquest?

Later, after enduring the indignity of learning to bathe myself in human fashion—and, worse, requiring Olivier's guidance to extricate myself from the bathing bin—I was given clothing. The weight of it felt foreign against my skin, each layer a reminder of my displacement.

Jonah's bed was warm. Unfamiliar, but not unkind. My body, still aching from the transformation's cruelty, surrendered to its softness. I barely had time to think before sleep dragged me under.

I woke to voices that slipped through the thin wooden walls.

"I do not know what he endured," Olivier was saying. "His mind seems misplaced, but I am certain he belongs to your missing fleet. I found him wandering—practically naked, save for this."

A shadow of unease coiled in my stomach. I sat up abruptly, hands searching the bedding. *Where is it?* The torn fragment of the ship—proof of what had happened, of what I had lost.

In my haste, my hand struck the cup beside the bed. It tumbled to the floor with a dull thunk.

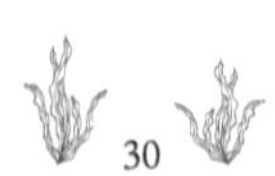

Beyond the doorway, Olivier's voice softened. "Ah. He's awake."

The door eased open, and Olivier stepped into view. His expression was unreadable, but his words came with quiet certainty.

"Rylen," he said, "I believe I've found your men." A pause, measured and deliberate. "You could have told me you were part of the missing fleet. I would have ridden through the night to bring you to them."

The air in the room thinned.

Perhaps this was the current that would carry me to the palace—to the King of Gadimore, and to the prince whose heart Morvena had claimed as her own.

Chapter Three

"Captain Roland LeVesque's fleet was due two mornings past. We feared the worst, and it seems we were right."

The Coastal Guard's voice was steady, though there was a weight behind it—a grief unspoken, a knowing that all who travel the sea must eventually pay its toll. And rightfully so. He cast a glance over his shoulder, meeting my gaze briefly before returning his focus to the road ahead. I tightened my grip around his waist, though the action was more necessity than comfort.

By the sea, I would have traded anything for the wooden vessel Olivier had tethered to his horse. Why did humans choose to ride these beasts? The creature beneath us was a mass of shifting muscle and barely restrained force, each jolt of its stride a fresh torment. Every time its hooves struck the earth, I could feel the impact in my bones.

My forehead knocked against the cold metal of the man's back—armor. A cage for the flesh, stiff and cumbersome, yet they seemed to wear it with ease. The other rider bore the same metallic shell, the plates catching flashes of daylight as we moved. Did the land hold such constant dangers that they must swaddle themselves in steel? Or was it merely the nature of men to prepare for war, even when no enemy loomed on the horizon?

"What was it that claimed them?" the man in front of me continued. "Pirates? A storm? Or one of the sea's cursed beasts?"

I did not answer.

"Enough," the second rider interjected, his tone curt. "We wait for the Fleet Admiral. He will have his own questions."

I exhaled slowly, relief unfurling in my chest. I had not yet thought of the words I would weave, the tale I would spin to fit their world. Perhaps I could stretch this silence until I stood before the King himself. If there was water near, I would not need another weapon. The sea had gifted me with weapons of its own. I could drown him where he stood. It would be a fitting end.

But what if the prince was there?

Morvena had warned me—his soul was touched by chaos. That meant power. Not as vast as the seawitch's, surely, but potent in ways I did not yet understand. And power rooted in the land would always have the advantage here, just as mine ruled absolute beneath the waves.

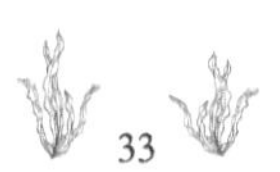

The road stretched on, dust rising beneath the pounding hooves. Ahead, a city loomed, its walls a pale defiance against the sky. And beyond them, the palace. The place where I would see his debt repaid.

The trees thinned, their wild embrace yielding to an expanse of stone, towering structures rising where the sky once reigned free. The scent of brine faded beneath an onslaught of new scents—woodsmoke and roasted flesh, something bitter, something cloyingly sweet. The world was louder here, voices overlapping in a cacophony of bartering and bickering, clatter against stone, the rhythmic pound of metal on metal. The path beneath the horse's hooves had hardened, no longer the soft bumpy, yielding earth of the path leading here.

Buildings loomed on either side, taller than Olivier's home, pressed together as though they sought warmth from each other. Some had signs hanging above their doors, marked with strange symbols I could not decipher, but others bore the likeness of objects—bread, a chalice, a fish—perhaps for those who could not read.

People swarmed like schools of fish, yet their movements were jarring, lacking the instinctive grace of the sea. They did not flow together but moved in jagged patterns, weaving around each other with sharp glances and muttered curses. Their garments varied—some draped in fine fabrics, their fingers heavy with glinting metal, while others wore patched and threadbare cloth, their faces drawn with weariness. Even on land, it seemed, there were those who ruled and those who merely survived.

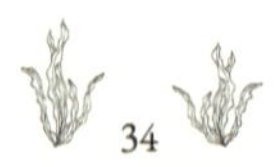

The walls of the buildings grew grander the deeper we rode into the city. Towers clawed at the sky, their tops vanishing into the low-hanging clouds. The air here carried something different—less smoke, more damp stone, the scent of something polished and metallic.

And then, the distance closed. The fortress of pale stone, its towers crowned with banners that caught in the wind like the unfurled fins of a great beast. Walls surrounded it, high and unyielding, lined with figures of metal and cloth—guards, armed and waiting.

Gratitude swelled within me as my boots touched the stone ground at last, solid and steady beneath me. The rhythmic clatter of hooves faded as palace guards stepped forward, taking the reins and leading the beasts away with murmured words of reassurance. The two Coastal Guards flanked me as we crossed into the castle, their presence a silent weight at my back.

The Aserian palace was a marvel of coral and currents, of shimmering halls that moved with the sea's breath. This human stronghold was different—solid, unyielding, yet no less grand. The vast archways and ceilings loomed overhead, traced with intricate carvings of twisting vines and beasts unknown to me. Stained glass windows framed the corridors, spilling jeweled colors across passing figures and the polished floors, the effect not unlike sunlight filtering through the waves.

I was led into a chamber, its purpose clear: a place of counsel, of strategy. A great wooden table dominated the space, unfurled across it a map—landmasses scrawled in dark ink, the

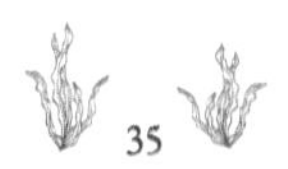

sprawl of Aserian among them. My gaze lingered there, tracing the familiar contours of my waters transcribed in a human hand.

"I will send for a physician," one of the guards said, motioning to a large chair. I sank into it, the fabric yielding beneath me, softer than I expected.

The other lingered near the entryway, arms resting at his sides, his presence an unspoken command to wait. My gaze drifted to the wide windows, my fingers tracing the smoothed edges of the talisman. The sky stretched vast and clear, the sun's warmth a ghostly caress against my skin. I wondered if my absence had been noted. Did my parents know? Had they already discerned my path, or did they believe I wandered as I always had—to distant currents, to distant kin, ever drawn by the quiet call of the sea?

The quiet hum of my thoughts was interrupted by approaching footsteps, deliberate and unhurried. A man entered, his attire plain compared to the finery I had glimpsed in the halls. A pair of delicate glass disks perched on the bridge of his nose, catching the light as he adjusted them. In one hand, he carried a leather bag, its weight pulling against his arm.

"Mathis de Clairvaux," the older gentleman introduced himself, extending a hand toward me. I curled my fingers tighter around the talisman, my brows pulling together.

He hesitated, scrutinizing me for a brief moment before turning to the guard who had escorted him.

"This is Rylen," the man explained. "A farmer from Harlowe found him in the middle of the road, not far from the

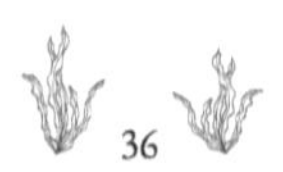

sea. He was naked, drenched, and smelled as if he had been adrift for days. His mind seems... off."

"Scurvy?" Mathis inquired, his composure settling into something practiced, assured. He stepped closer, his gaze flicking back to me. "Rylen, was it?"

I gave a stiff nod.

"I need to check for signs of ailment." He set his bag beside me, and before I could react, his fingers were in my mouth, prying my lips apart.

I jerked, a startled sound caught in my throat.

"Gums are healthy," he murmured, tilting my head slightly. "Teeth—normal."

I swatted at his hand, my patience fraying. "Stop."

This was undignified. I was a prince. No one had ever subjected me to such crude examinations before.

Unbothered, Mathis pressed on. "He doesn't appear dehydrated," he observed, lifting the hem of my shirt without permission. "Nor malnourished."

He spoke as though I were not present, merely an object to be assessed.

"No sores." He took my chin firmly in hand, leaning closer to inspect me. "No external head trauma."

I struck his hand away again, my temper snapping. "Do not touch me," I hissed.

He met my glare with an impassive one of his own before straightening. "Some men return from the sea changed," he mused, as if diagnosing an affliction beyond flesh and bone.

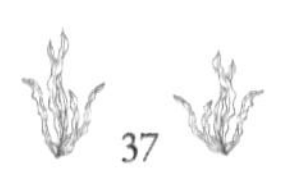

"It lingers in them—the things they have seen, what they have endured. It takes time to unmoor them from it."

He turned to the guards, as if I were no longer a participant in the conversation. "Rest, Saint John's Wort in his morning tea, lemons in the evening before bed. And daily confessionals with the clergy, so that he may unburden himself of whatever troubles the sea has left upon him."

I stared at him. Madness. Utter madness. Yet the guards nodded solemnly, as though his words held undeniable truth.

Another figure entered the room, his presence shifting the air itself. His hands rested casually behind his back, yet there was nothing idle in the way he carried himself. His stride was not light, nor hesitant, but strong, commanding. Authority laced his every movement, making my spine straighten instinctively.

Mathis bowed at once, his voice reverent. "Your Highness."

The two Coastal Guards followed suit, inclining their heads in swift acknowledgment. "Admiral."

He was broader than the others, his frame built for the weight of command, yet there was an undeniable softness to his features. The way dark locks framed his face, the gentle curve of his lips as he spoke. It was a contradiction—a figure carved for war with a face meant for song. His attire spoke of that very sentiment. At his hip, metal lay sheathed in leather, a human weapon forged for the swift deliverance of death. Upon his head, more metal, shaped not for function or protection but for spectacle, curved in such a way that it became art—an unspoken declaration that this was a man meant to be revered.

"Who is this?" His gaze flicked to me, then back to the men.

"A fisherman, Olivier Fenais of Harlowe, found him," one of the guards answered. "We suspect he may have been part of Captain LeVesque's fleet."

Mathis leaned in, his voice hushed, as if sharing some damning secret. "He has been afflicted with madness, Your Majesty."

The admiral stepped closer, his body lowering until we were eye to eye. And for the first time, I saw them clearly—his eyes. A green so rich, so deep, it was like the sea itself had stilled and turned to glass. Emeralds in the light.

This was him.

This was the prince she spoke of.

"What is your name?" he asked, his voice a study in gentleness, his expression open.

I tilted my head, studying him in turn. Those eyes, that look—I had seen them before. Somewhere beyond memory, beyond reason. The talisman slipped from my grasp, forgotten, as my hand lifted of its own accord.

My fingers brushed his jaw, then cupped his face, tracing warmth where I expected cold.

The guards moved instantly, the sound of metal shifting, bodies tensing.

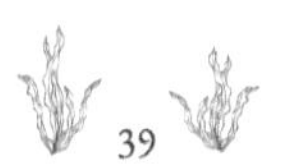

But the prince did not retreat. He did not flinch from my touch. He merely raised a hand—not to me, but to them. A silent command.

"Who are you?" I whispered.

His fingers curled around my wrist, his hold careful, steadying.

"Titus," he said.

Titus.

The memory struck like a wave, pulling me under.

A woman's voice, distant yet clear—"Prince Titus, come, we must head back to the palace. The carriage awaits you."

"Coming, one moment!" The boy called back, his voice bright with impatience. But his gaze lingered on me, torn between duty and the wonder that held him here. He glanced over his shoulder, past the rocky outcroppings that shielded us from prying eyes, before turning back, his face alight with curiosity.

"What about crabs? Can they talk, or is it similar to the fishes, where you just know what they're trying to say?"

I chuckled. "Crabs are the same. All creatures of the sea speak their own special language. It is the language of the sea."

"Can you teach me?" His eyes were so wide, so eager.

"It's not that simple. Not like how you and I are speaking. Or how I would speak to another mer." A smile tugged at my lips.

"What about holding my breath for a long time?" He sucked in air, puffing out his cheeks, jabbing a stick into the

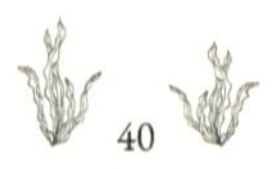

sand palace we had built. Shells slid from its wet towers, cascading down like fallen stars. He exhaled sharply, his voice strained. "Can you teach me that?"

"I do not need to hold my breath. I have these." I tilted my head, fingers brushing over the delicate slits of my gills.

His hesitation was brief, a quiet reverence in his movements as he reached out—not for himself, but for me.

"Can I?"

I nodded, baring my neck. His touch was light, barely there, yet filled with such intent. His fingers traced along my skin, careful, fascinated.

"Incredible," he breathed. His awe shone brighter than the sun on the water's surface.

"Your Highness!" The woman's voice, closer now.

Titus flinched, then sighed, reluctant. "I have to go." His lips pursed, his small face creased with disappointment. "Will I see you again?"

I hesitated. "I hope so."

"Five sunrises from now. Swear to it. Right here."

I bent down, dipping my fingers into the shallows, tracing the sand until I found what I sought. A shell, smooth and pale, kissed by the tides. "A mer's promise." I pressed it into his palm. "Five sunrises. Same place."

He held it as if it were sacred. "A mer's promise?" he echoed, voice hushed, reverent.

"Prince Titus!"

"Five sunrises," he vowed, scrambling to his feet. He clutched the shell to his chest, grinning as he turned to climb

the rocks. His small frame silhouetted against the sky, the damp fabric clinging to him, his footprints left to the mercy of the tide. He stopped once more, looking down at me.

"Don't forget!"

"I won't!" I called back, laughter on my lips, the salt wind at my back.

The memory receded like the tide, leaving behind only the ache of its absence.

He had not returned as he said.

"Rylen," I answered at last.

He repeated my name, tasting it, testing it. No flicker of recognition crossed his face. No spark of remembrance in those green eyes. I swallowed, my hand slipping away from Titus, from the man before me who no longer carried the boy I had once known.

He had forgotten me. Perhaps it was for the best. But I would be a liar if I said it did not send a sharp, cold pain through my chest.

"What happened to you?" he asked. "Where is Captain LeVesque?"

"I do not know," I murmured, my gaze drifting from him, seeking refuge in the map spread across the table. It called to me as if I could slip between those lines, return to the currents that bore me, to the sanctuary of salt and silence.

Instead, I remained here, ensnared by the weight of duty and the quiet, creeping ache of something foolish, something I should not feel.

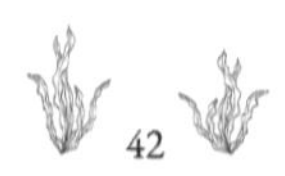

Why had I thought—hoped—that he might remember? That he might be anything other than what he was? A human. A creature of the land. A thing meant to disappoint and destroy. He was, after all, the one who commanded the humans that invaded my seas. He was no longer the curious, wide-eyed child I once knew... and neither was I.

"What do you know?" His voice was gentle, careful, as though I might break apart at the seams if he pressed too hard. He was coaxing me to meet his gaze, to fall into the depths of those beautiful eyes that had once known me.

I did not.

"None survived but me." The words left my lips with more force than I had intended, brittle with conviction, edged with something else—something jagged and unspoken.

Hatred.

Mathis leaned in then, his voice lowered in an imitation of discretion, though he made no true effort to keep his words from me. As if I were not capable of understanding. As if I were some mad thing to be tempered.

"Your Highness, this is good. Continue to speak with him. It will bring him out of his madness sooner if he converses and confides with someone he trusts."

My madness? I nearly laughed. If there was madness in this room, surely it was Mathis who suffered from it.

Titus said nothing, only studied me as though he could read through the layers of silence between us. Then, slowly, cautiously, his hand extended toward me, his fingers brushing the torn scrap of sail I had bound around my waist like a sash.

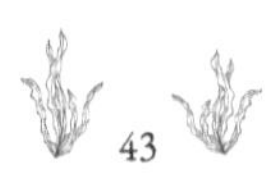

I tensed.

"What did this?" he asked. "Who did this?"

The scent of the sea clung to it, thick in my lungs. "I—I do not remember." The words wavered as I shrank back into the seat, retreating from him with nowhere to go.

Titus hesitated, his fingers curling slightly before he withdrew his hand.

"Make ready a guest chamber for Rylen," he said, his voice composed, unreadable. "He will remain until he is able to recount what happened to Captain LeVesque's fleet."

One of the guards bowed and left without a word.

Titus lingered a moment longer, his gaze steady, searching. Before he could take another step away, I spoke.

"Where is your king?"

Titus paused, his shoulder grazing the frame of the door as he turned back to me. His posture remained easy, almost careless, yet there was a sharpness to his gaze.

"King Beaumir? My father?" A slight tilt of his head. "Why? Have you recalled something urgent about the fleet?"

"No... No." The words came slower this time, measured. "Your physician suggested I speak with someone I trust. I trust your king."

The lie curdled on my tongue, thick as brine. As if I would ever trust any of them. These men of the land, with their iron and their hunger, their hands forever outstretched in conquest.

But Titus only nodded, as if the notion made perfect sense. "I see. That is reasonable." His lips quirked into

something like amusement, an expression light and understanding. "My father is away in Balthvidae and is expected to return in seven mornings. I will arrange for you to speak with him upon his return."

Seven mornings.

My fingers drifted to the talisman, tracing its edges, as if I could feel the magic dwindling with every breath I stole from this air. Morvena had warned me—the chaos would bleed away, leeched from my bones the longer I lingered. If I left, if I rejoined the sea, even for a breath, perhaps I could weave more time into my illusion. Perhaps I would not fade before I reached the man I came to kill.

Titus watched me still. The weight of his gaze settled over me, burning through the pretense I wore. It was the way a man looks at something just out of reach. Did he remember me?

"I do not remember you."

The words were quiet, yet they landed like a blade against my ribs.

"It weighs heavily on me," he continued. "As Admiral, I should know all the men in my fleet. But your name, your face—they escape me. I must apologize, Rylen. I will do better."

"Oh."

A simple word, an empty one, yet it was all I could force past my lips.

Titus did not linger. He turned with easy grace, stepping into the corridor beyond. Mathis followed, his gait less

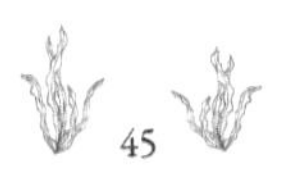

fluid, stiff with the air of a man who thought himself important.

"Come, Rylen." The remaining guard gestured for me to rise. "The Chamberlain will see you settled while you recover."

I let him lead me through the palace halls. If they believed me broken, then I would play the part until King Beaumir returned.

We moved through the palace, past a gathering of humans draped in the muted finery of their station—attendants, servants, those who bent their spines beneath the weight of those above them. Their presence whispered of function rather than form, their gazes averted as the Coastal Guard and I passed.

"Elisienne," he called, and the cluster of bodies parted like a tide pulled by the moon, leaving one woman standing alone.

She was worn unlike the others. Though time had yet to carve its claim into her, it lingered at the edges, waiting. Her brown hair was drawn high, smooth and severe, a deliberate act of order. Soft honey eyes regarded me, patient, unreadable. Her hands lay poised at her abdomen, fingers neatly folded.

"Sir." Her head dipped, a gesture I recognized as respect.

"This is Rylen..." The guard hesitated, his gaze flicking to me. "I do not believe I caught your family name?"

Family name. A peculiar human invention, to carry the weight of one's lineage in syllables. We merfolk had no such

burden—our names belonged to the sea, to the currents that whispered them into existence.

"Aseria," I said at last, reaching for the only thing that my weary mind could grasp.

The guard nodded, satisfied, and turned back to Elisienne. "Rylen Aseria. One of the missing men from Captain LeVesque's fleet."

"Ah," she murmured, her eyes drifting to me once more. A slight dip of her chin, an acknowledgment rather than a greeting. "So this is the man they whisper of."

"He is to remain within these walls under the orders of Prince Titus and Lord Mathis de Clairvaux. See that he is tended to."

"Yes, sir." She inclined her head once more before shifting her gaze to me. "Right this way, Rylen. I will show you to your quarters."

I followed, silent as she led me through the vast and excessive corridors of human opulence. The walls bore their past—portraits of rulers, long dead yet preserved in pigment and gilded frame, their gazes hollow and watching. Some had been given permanence in stone, their features chiseled into something cold and unyielding. There were halls for dining, for gathering, for feasting, for ruling, each space dictated by purpose yet blending into excess.

"The great hall," she said, gesturing as we passed beneath a vaulted arch. "The throne room." A flick of her hand. "The royal library." Another turn. "The gardens beyond that corridor, the palace chapel through there."

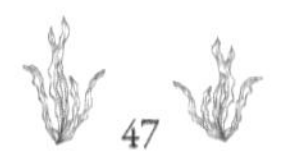

A divide loomed before us—a fork in the river of polished marble and filtered light.

"The wings," she explained. "East belongs to the crown, where the royal family resides. The west is for those granted the court's hospitality. You will stay there."

Wings. A word meant for flight, yet all I saw was further separation from those that ruled the land and those who served.

We continued down the west wing, the hush of our footfalls swallowed by the weight of the palace's silence. The corridor stretched before us, lined with doors of dark, polished wood, their gilded handles catching the glow of the sun filtering in from outside.

At last, our path ended.

"This will be your chamber," Elisienne said, pausing before an arched doorway. The door swung open at her touch, revealing the space that would serve as my prison—my gilded cage until the tide shifted in my favor.

The room was vast, but its grandeur felt stifling rather than indulgent. Heavy drapes of deep indigo spilled from the towering windows, their embroidered edges sweeping the polished floor like waves caught mid-crest. The walls, paneled in rich mahogany, bore carvings of intertwining vines, a mockery of something living, something untamed. Glistening crystal hung above, refracting firelight into scattered fragments that danced across the ceiling like shattered stars.

A great bed stood at the heart of it all, draped in fine linens of navy and silver, its canopy cascading in sheer fabric

that trembled at the slightest breath of air. Too much space. Too much softness. The ocean had never cradled me so. This was stifling.

A table rested against the far wall, adorned with tools and parchments. A hearth lay unlit, its carved stone mantle a testament to the humans' endless war against the cold.

To the right, a door stood slightly ajar, revealing a glimpse of a washing chamber. The scent of lavender lingered in the air, clinging to the tapestries, the linens, the very walls—as if the room had been soaked in it, drowning out any trace of those who had stayed before.

I stepped inside, the weight of it pressing against me. The sea was nowhere to be heard, no gentle lull of the tide, no whisper of waves against the shore. Only silence. Heavy, expectant, inescapable.

Elisienne watched me, unreadable aside for a hint of curiosity. "I shall see to it that you have all you need," she said. "If there is anything you require, you need only ask."

I did not answer. There was only one thing I required, and no human could grant it.

With a final nod, she took her leave, the door clicking shut behind her.

Alone, I exhaled, the sound too loud in the hush of the chamber. My fingers found the talisman at my throat, its cool weight grounding me. *Seven mornings.* There was no way I could remain here for that long.

My fingers trailed along the carved wood of the bed, as I turned to the window, letting my hands glide over the frame,

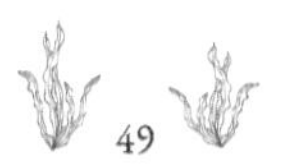

searching until I found the mechanism that yielded to my touch. The panes parted with a whisper, and a breath of cool air curled into the room, brushing against my skin.

I inhaled sharply, but the scent of the sea was faint, almost lost beneath the weight of earthbound things—stone and greenery, the damp musk of the river that ran sluggish through the capital. The waves were too far. The sound of them too distant, swallowed by the sprawling gardens below, by the walls that loomed high and cruel against the horizon.

My gaze swept downward. The earth stretched beneath me in a tapestry of humans moving in their quiet, purposeful patterns. Servants, courtiers, soldiers—all playing their roles beneath the shadow of their ruler's hand. Among them, small creatures darted—foxes slinking through the underbrush, mice scurrying between cracks in the stone, birds flitting to the safety of branches. Everything here lived with the constant awareness of a predator's presence.

I was no different.

Pulling a chair to the window, I curled into its depths, letting its unnatural softness cradle me as I watched the evening unfold. My eyes traced the figures below until their movements blurred, until the weight of exhaustion pressed heavily against my limbs. The world faded into the hush of twilight, into the lull of distant voices and the cool kiss of the wind against my cheek.

A sharp knock pulled me from the haze of sleep.

I stiffened, pressing back into the chair's embrace as the door creaked open.

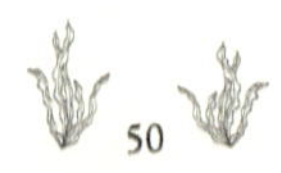

Titus stood in the threshold, the waning light casting long shadows across his form. In his hands, he turned a small yellow sphere idly between his fingers, the movement slow, measured. "I hope I am not disturbing you," he said, though there was no apology in his tone.

I glanced back to the window. The sky had deepened into a rich violet, the last traces of sunlight burning at the edges of the horizon. How long had I slept?

When I did not speak, his gaze flickered down to the object in his hands. "Elisienne was meant to bring this to you and then escort you to the chapel for confession," he continued. "Mathis insists it will aid in your recovery." A pause, his voice turning almost light, as if the words were something less than an order. "I was heading that way myself. I thought I might accompany you."

"*Continue to speak with him. It will bring him out of his madness sooner if he converses and confides in someone he trusts.*" Mathis' words echoed through my mind, curling like sea mist in the quiet.

This was not kindness.

The prince had not come to offer comfort, nor out of some misplaced sense of duty. This was yet another method of extraction—retrieval cloaked in the guise of recovery. A delicate deception, wrapped in gentleness, in quiet patience, in the illusion of trust.

Were they always this deceitful to their own kind? Did they make a habit of weaving softness around their lies, of

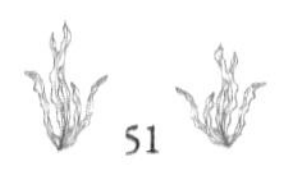

luring each other into vulnerability before sinking in their hooks?

Perhaps I was not the only one playing a part.

I said nothing, only held out a hand, my gaze settling on the yellow sphere.

Titus stepped forward, placing it carefully in my palm.

It was lighter than I expected, its surface textured beneath my fingers, cool from the evening air. I turned it over, bringing it closer, inhaling its scent. There was something bright about it, something sharp—not the sweetness of flowers in bloom, but something cleaner, more distant. Like sunlight caught in the crest of a wave before it breaks.

"What is this?" I asked.

For the briefest moment, his expression shifted—his lips thinning, his brow barely creasing. A flicker of something unreadable. Then it was gone, replaced by the same practiced ease he seemed to always wear. "A lemon," he said. "Before bed. You remember, don't you?"

"I am to eat this?" I arched a brow.

"Yes."

I hesitated and lifted the lemon once more, studying the way the light glowed faintly against its dimpled skin.

Titus watched me, expectant.

I raised it to my lips and bit down.

The bitterness of the flesh struck first, waxy and acrid, clinging to my tongue like the taste of something spoiled. Then the wetness beneath—an explosion of acid, searing and ruthless, flooding my mouth with a sharpness that made my

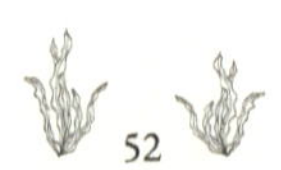

jaw ache. It was not like the salt of the sea, nor the sweetness of blooms I had known in the deep. It was something else entirely, something violent in its contrast. My throat clenched as I forced myself to swallow, my lips curling in instinctive revulsion.

"That is horrid," I rasped, dropping the lemon to the floor as if it had personally wronged me. My tongue flicked against my teeth, desperate to rid itself of the offense, but the taste lingered, stubborn as barnacles on a ship's hull.

Titus chuckled as he bent down, retrieving the fallen lemon with the ease of someone who had expected this outcome. He placed it upon the table, amusement still flickering in his expression.

"Well, it is a sour thing," he said, as if that were an excuse for such an abomination. "And you are supposed to rid yourself of the peel first too."

"Sour?" I repeated, my brow furrowing. "Peel?"

His laughter faded, though the curiosity remained. He studied me then, his gaze sweeping over my face, searching for something—some explanation, perhaps. Something that did not add up.

I did not move, did not let my expression betray me. The silence between us stretched, weighty and uncertain, before he finally spoke.

"Your mind is an oblivious thing right now isn't it," he murmured. Not a question, but a quiet realization.

My gaze lingered on him, searching, measuring. A quiet breath left my lips as I stood, stepping forward. "Take me to

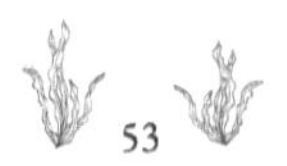

this confession that must be made," I said, the words slipping out like a command dressed in civility.

His lips quirked, something like amusement ghosting across his expression as he folded his arms over his broad chest.

Standing this close, I noticed—though his frame was larger, his presence heavier—we were near equal in height. But that was where our similarities ended. Strength pooled beneath his garments, the fabric taut where his arms flexed with even the smallest shift of posture. It was a warrior's body, shaped by discipline, carved by conflict.

A sliver of unease curled in my gut. At the end of all this, I would need to take this prince's heart. A task simple in words, but if it was true that he was touched by chaos, then I was outmatched—not only in strength but in magic. I did not possess the arrogance to deny that. The sea willing, my mind would prove sharper than any weapon, my steps more cunning than his own. I prayed, not for an easy hunt, but for survival.

"Of course, Rylen," he said at last, breaking the silence before it could settle too deeply between us. "Right this way."

The palace had quieted, its earlier bustle dulled to a hush. The only figures haunting the halls now were men clad in metal, standing as still as statues, their gazes forward, their purpose singular. The air carried the scent of burning oil, the flickering glow of firelight pooling across the marble—contained, harnessed, strung up in iron frames that clung to the walls.

We came upon a set of great doors, the ones Elisienne had gestured to before. The entrance to their chapel. With a mere murmur of, *Your Highness*, the guards unbarred the way, the doors groaning as they parted.

Inside, the space yawned wide and empty. Cold, hollow, a cavern of human reverence.

The stone figures lining the corridors had been varied, many, but this one—this one loomed larger, grander. A man carved in pale stone, flesh hewn from rock, standing sentinel at the room's heart on a pedestal. Unlike the others, this figure was near bare, his body only partially obscured by a carefully draped fold of stone, shielding what I supposed were his reproductive parts. I was grateful for it.

Titus strode forward, the sound of his boots swallowed by the vastness of the chamber. Along the outer perimeter of the room, slender waxen objects stood in solemn rows, their flames flickering, casting a warm but wavering dimness upon the stone. He reached for one upon a nearby ledge, fingers curling around its smooth body, its crown marked by a thread of blackened wick.

"Mind the candles," he mused, holding it between his fingers. "A fire hazard, in my opinion, but no one can argue with the clergy. Or at least, I tried to argue—for sconces, for braziers, even a damned chandelier."

I frowned, my teeth catching briefly on the inside of my lip as my gaze dropped to the object in his hands.

I had seen them before—these small sticks of wax arranged in clusters, their tops burned and blackened. A display

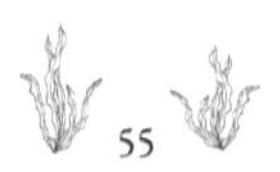

of how humans had harnessed the sun's light with their chaos, bending it to their will. Sometimes encased in metal, sometimes bound to wood, and now, molded into wax. Unnatural illumination, defying the dark, keeping their world awake when it should be sleeping. But I had not questioned them, nor thought to name them.

He lifted it slightly. "A candle," he said, his voice softer now, the word shaped with an absent sort of care. "It burns, gives light. And, in unfortunate circumstances, takes it away."

I extended my hand, drawn by the quiet lure of the flame. Its warmth licked at my skin, not yet touching, but close enough that I could feel its breath against my fingers. Before I could reach it—before I could test the heat for myself—a hand closed around my wrist. Firm, but not unkind. My gaze lifted, meeting his.

"Don't," Titus murmured. A simple word, but edged with something cautionary, something almost—concerned. "You'll harm yourself if you touch it."

Slowly, I withdrew, but the ghost of his touch lingered longer than the candlelight. It was warmer than the fire, more present. A strange thing. My eyes drifted from him to the vast chamber, to the long wooden seats that lined its hollowed expanse, rigid and unyielding. They were arranged with a quiet order, rows upon rows, facing the figure that loomed at the chamber's heart.

Titus moved between them, stepping with a reverence I had not yet seen in him. He knelt before the stone figure, its expression fixed in eternal serenity.

"Valtherion," he intoned, placing the candle at the foot of the carved man. "A god. He embodies greatness and power through virtue. Those who live virtuously are believed to be blessed with wisdom, strength, and mastery of the arcane."

A pause. "Lord de Clairvaux believes that if you speak to Valtherion, he will mend what has been broken within you. Restore the wisdom and strength you once had before the sea."

My steps carried me forward, echoing across stone. "What of the arcane?"

Titus turned slightly, brow creasing. "Arcane?"

"You said this god blesses those worthy with wisdom and strength," I said, eyes fixed upon the stone man, its features crafted with an elegance too precise to be human. "But you also said he offers mastery of the arcane. Is that not something to be restored as well?"

"Well, are you an arcanist?"

I stopped beside him, standing above where he knelt, watching as the candlelight licked at his silhouette. He lifted his gaze to mine, searching, though I offered no spoken answer—only silence, only the weight of my stare. It seemed to suffice.

With measured ease, he rose, his expression untouched by irritation or impatience. Only quiet neutrality remained. Then, softly, he extended his hand toward me.

"May I have your hand?"

I hesitated, then gave it to him. He turned it gently, my palm resting upward in his grasp, his fingers tracing lightly across the lines etched into my skin. The warmth of his touch

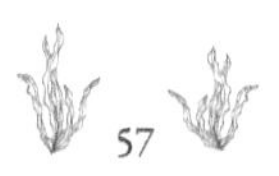

was peculiar, tingling, leaving a sensation that settled somewhere deeper than flesh. Again and again, he repeated the motion, until something began to take shape beneath his fingers—marks, dark and unreadable, foreign to my eyes. And then, the ink lifted.

I stilled.

It twisted, unraveling from my skin, reshaping itself into orbs of light—small at first, shifting, coalescing. He leaned in, exhaling a breath against my palm, warm as summer air. The candles throughout the chamber extinguished in unison, swallowed by darkness. And in their place, the light he had drawn from me scattered, drifting upward, growing, becoming something vast, something luminous.

Starlight.

He had conjured starlight within these hallowed walls.

One word slipped from my lips, reverent, awed. "Chaos."

I had only ever been told of its ruinous nature—of how it burned, corrupted, twisted the world to its will. But this—this was something else entirely. Something untainted, something impossibly beautiful.

"I am an arcanist," he murmured, releasing my hand. "This is arcane."

I raised my fingers, reaching, trying to grasp the light he had breathed into existence. But when I touched it, there was nothing. Only air, empty and undisturbed. And yet, I could feel it—the hum of power, the pull of something unseen, something not unlike what surrounded Morvena.

Beside me, Titus exhaled, his gaze still fixed upon the drifting light. "Illusions," he murmured, almost to himself. "Beautiful, but not real."

"How…" I swallowed, still watching as the stars flickered, shifting in and out of themselves like a mirage upon the waves. "How did you do that?"

"I told you—I am an arcanist."

"But how?"

His eyes flickered toward the god of stone. "It is believed that Valtherion blesses certain bloodlines with the ability to harness the arcane. Beaumir is one of them."

"So it cannot be learned?"

"No." A quiet sigh escaped him. "Some are born with it, some are not. You can only pray that he will bless your lineage—or help you sharpen the gifts you already possess."

Valtherion. The god of humans. The one who chose who was touched by chaos, whose blood would carry the weight of it. But how had Morvena known? How had she traced this gift to him, to this specific man? And if she had known—how had she harnessed it?

Titus raised a hand, fingers moving through the air in an absent, practiced gesture. The stars flickered, then vanished.

Darkness swelled in their place, thick and absolute. But it did not last. One by one, the candles began to rekindle, their flames emerging from the shadows, small and delicate at first, before rising to their full, flickering height—restoring the room to what it once was.

"Show me more," I said, turning to face him, my voice a quiet plea wrapped in command.

Titus arched a brow, the faintest curl of amusement tugging at his mouth. "Does the word please not exist in your vocabulary? You are rather a bold one—and to a prince, no less."

The words struck not cruelly, but with a certain smug refinement, like a metal kissed with silk. I faltered, realizing my misstep. Here, I was not a prince beneath the sea, no heir woven from tide and song—I was a displaced creature wrapped in a stranger's skin, a curiosity teetering on the edge of disdain. To him, I was not royalty. Merely something meant to serve and be commanded.

"...Please," I murmured, the word tasting foreign on my tongue. "Show me more."

He inclined his head, gracious as a sovereign accepting tribute. "Thank you," he said, voice softened into velvet. "I shall—should you offer me something in return. Knowledge of the fleet, perhaps. And if you possess none, then obedience to Mathis' orders will suffice. If I am to be your diversion, it must be earned. Do we understand each other?"

There was no edge to his tone, only the calm assurance of one accustomed to being obeyed. I nodded, once.

"Then you may choose—answers, or confession."

He did not wait for me to speak. He already knew which I would choose. With measured grace, he knelt once more before the stone deity.

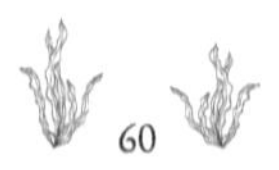

I followed, slower this time, sinking down beside him as the silence stretched like a hush drawn across water. He bowed his head. Eyes closed. Still.

Was this part of the confessing? Was I meant to mimic him?

"I..." My voice trembled into the hush, barely audible. "I do not understand what it is I am meant to do here."

He did not look at me. "Speak to Valtherion," he said, soft as dusk. "Tell him what weighs upon you. Guilt, anger, sorrow, longing—whatever festers, whatever burns. Or joy, if you can still recall the shape of it."

"Will he answer?"

"Sometimes," Titus said, after a pause. "When it is needed. But more often, it is the unburdening that matters. To place your grief in the hands of something that does not judge."

I watched him, carefully. The quiet lines of his face. The steadiness of his breath. He seemed so composed, so unwavering. Yet something within me whispered—what did he have to confess? What wounds did he carry in silence, buried beneath patience and kindness?

The questions curled inside me, restless and aching. Perhaps I only wanted to know because it made what I would one day have to do easier. Perhaps I needed something to crush the echo of the boy I once knew—needed to forget the kindness that lingered still in his eyes.

I turned my gaze to the stone god and closed my eyes, pressing my thoughts into the dark behind them.

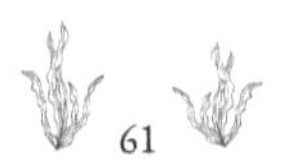

Ail me, I begged, the words not spoken but felt. Give me a reason to hate him. Give me the grace to carry out what I must—without regret.

Chapter Four

Elisienne guided me to the small table carved with gilded flourishes and crowned with a mirror—a vanity, she had called it. I was learning there were dozens of words for what should have been one thing. Desks. Trestles. Dining tables. Humans seemed to find comfort in excess, in fracturing the simple into a thousand delicate names.

In the reflection, I watched her draw back the heavy drapes. Morning spilled in, soft and golden. The breeze stirred the air like a sigh, and I felt it ghost over my skin—a sweetness I could not name and the distant scent of horses and stone. I had been too weary last night to steal away to the sea, too drained from whatever magic Titus had pressed into the air between us.

I traced the rim of the blue glass resting against my chest. It hadn't changed. No sign yet that it would return to what it once was.

Elisienne's voice stirred the air behind me, gentle, tentative. "Forgive me if I speak out of turn, but… you're not from Gadimore, are you?"

My gaze met hers in the mirror, my blue against her honeyed. I said nothing. I didn't need to.

She offered a small smile as her fingers began to unweave the plaits from my hair. One by one, the strands fell free, dark and silken, spilling past my shoulders like inky midnight drawn into water.

"It's your hair… and this," she added, her fingers brushing the adornment at my ear—metal, sea glass, shell. "It's unlike the fashion here. For men. Or even women."

She opened a small wooden box, fingers selecting a strange tool from within. Bristles fanned from its base. A brush, I remembered. She raised it delicately. "Would you like me to style it differently? Something… more fitting. More masculine?"

I turned my head slightly, meeting her eyes again through the mirror's veil. "More masculine?" I echoed, unfamiliar with the shape of the word.

"Manly," she explained, gently. "Like a man." Her tone was cautious, as if she sensed the slight shift in my breath, the tension she had unknowingly summoned.

"My appearance does not unmake me a man," I said, voice low, measured. "I wish to remain as I am."

A flush touched her cheeks. "Of course, sir. I meant no disrespect." She lowered her eyes and set to brushing my hair. The strokes were slow, methodical, and almost admiring. "It's only that… others may think you are…" She faltered, gesturing

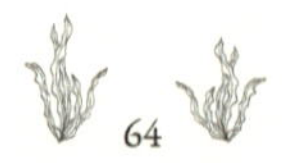

vaguely with the brush, struggling to shape the word in a way I'd understand. Her accent thickened, foreign vowels sliding into the air. "Effeminate. One who... indulges in sodomy."

My brows furrowed, not in offense, but confusion.

She clarified, delicately: "That you lay with other men. It is not... accepted here. You will be treated differently if they believe so. As something less. Less than a woman, even."

Less than a woman. How cruel humans could be. Their hierarchies were not only woven from power and bloodlines, but from flesh—what shape it took, whom it touched. The scale of worth decided not by honor or soul, but by the direction of one's longing.

"I do not care how your people perceive me," I said at last. The words were not armor. They were truth.

Elisienne paused, her eyes finding mine in the mirror again, softer now. "And you shouldn't," she said. "People ought to be judged by what they do. Or by what they refuse to do."

She resumed brushing, her silence not submission, but respect. The kind of quiet that allowed thoughts to stretch, uncoil, and breathe.

A knock came—soft, tentative. The door cracked open before permission could be granted, and a figure slipped inside. He was young—hovering in that fragile space between boyhood and manhood—shoulders narrow, posture folded with servitude. In his hands, a tray trembled faintly with the weight of porcelain and expectation.

He did not speak. Eyes lowered, he crossed the chamber and placed the cup gently upon the vanity, the sound a whisper against the wood.

So many hands, all doing the work of one. A small task fractured, dispersed. In Aserian, we ruled—but we were never above. Nobility was not a crown of gold but a mantle of obligation. We served as much as we reigned. We protected. We advocated. And if we failed, we were cast into the tide and replaced by those more worthy. We knew our power was borrowed, not bestowed.

"Thank you," I murmured as the boy retreated, slipping through the door like a ghost unsure of its welcome.

Elisienne's voice floated to me. "I believe that is the tea Lord Mathis wishes for you to have each morning."

I reached for the cup, lifting it. The porcelain was warm beneath my fingers, the heat subtle but constant, as though it pulsed with a life of its own. I raised it to my face.

The scent was sharp, earthy—like wet bark left too long in shadow. Beneath it, a whisper of something floral, nearly hidden, a sweetness that never dared to bloom.

I drank.

The taste struck bitter. Dry. Like old herbs crushed beneath a heel. It clung to my tongue with all the grace of ash. There was no comfort in it—only purpose. I swallowed it anyway.

I did not like this.

But Titus had made me a deal, and for now, I would play along. He said if I obeyed, he would show me more of his chaos. And I needed to see it again. I had to.

There had to be more to it than Valtherion's blessing. If all chaos was divine favor, how then had Morvena harnessed it? She had no altar, no whispered prayers. The humans gave reverence to many—gods of light and grain and war and knowledge—but we had only one.

The Sea.

It had never needed names or temples. It simply was. Terrible. Beautiful. Endless.

So where did Titus' magic come from? How did his fingers summon starlight, his breath extinguish flame? I needed answers. I needed a reason.

"Where is your prince?" I asked, though my tongue still bore the bitterness of the tea, the taste clinging like regret.

Elisienne gathered a length of my hair and began to twist it gently between her fingers. "Prince Titus usually confers with the fleet in the early morning. He trains after—swordwork, I believe. He returns to the palace only once the sun begins its descent. Did you wish an audience with him?"

"No."

Or perhaps I did.

What else was there to do in this gilded cage while King Beaumir was absent? At least Titus' presence served a purpose. Everyone else here was a name without weight—ornamentation in a world I was meant to unravel. Collateral dressed in velvet.

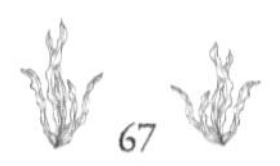

I shifted in my seat. "Am I allowed to leave this room?"

She blinked. "Yes? You've not been kept to it, only... restricted to the palace grounds. And not in the East Wing. No one aside from the royal guard is permitted there."

So I went to the East Wing.

Or rather, I attempted to.

The corridor yawned long and quiet, lit by a bloodless wash of morning light filtering through narrow stained-glass windows. But before I could step through its threshold, two guards blocked my path—silent, stiff, and unyielding. More lingered beyond them, armored shadows posted at regular intervals. Their silence spoke clearly enough.

Unwelcomed.

Thwarted, I turned away, feigning indifference, and wandered instead through a hall lined with painted panels and oil sconces, until I came upon a chamber whose doors had been left slightly ajar. The scent drew me first—aged parchment, brittle as coral, dust tinged with candle wax and ink. I stepped inside.

The chamber opened like a cavern—high ceilinged and breathless, its walls consumed by shelves that climbed toward domed stone. Wood, dark and polished, gleamed faintly beneath the lacework of morning shadow. Every surface was burdened with stacks—parchments curled at the edges, thick bound tomes with strange designs pressed into their hides, delicate scrolls sleeping within narrow compartments. It felt... reverent. Sacred, almost.

Though the marks inside meant nothing to me, I wandered the aisles still, letting my fingers graze over cracked parchment and timeworn spines, imagining what might lie within. Within some I found images—painted depictions of lands I had never seen, creatures rendered in strokes both delicate and monstrous.

"Do you like to read?"

The voice stirred the stillness like a vibration across calmed waters. I turned, startled, to find Titus leaning against a nearby shelf, arms loose at his sides, the corner of his mouth lifted ever so slightly.

"Pardon?" I asked, drawing my hand back from the leather binding as though it had burned me.

"I simply assumed one only enters a library if they enjoy reading," he replied, stepping forward to tap the spine of a thick tome. His fingers curved around it, pulling it free with practiced ease. "Books. These are vessels," he said. "Each one filled with voices. Wisdom, knowledge, fantasy—and, sometimes, more often than not, lies dressed up as truth."

"Books," I echoed softly.

He nodded. "This room is their sanctuary."

I turned back to the book beneath my hand and slid it free, opening it delicately. My fingers traced the dark ink. "I was told you wouldn't return until evening," I said, eyes still on the page.

"Were you waiting for me?" he asked, tone casual.

"No. Yes. I—no."

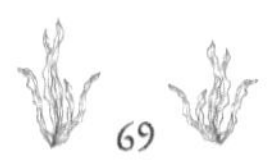

He slid the book he'd taken back into place. "Is there information you meant to give me, then?"

"No."

A pause. Then, a shift in his stance, arms folding across his chest. "How exactly did you come to know my schedule?"

"I overheard it," I lied—partially.

"Well, my father's absence means I must divide my time more evenly," he said. "So I'm here now. At your service."

Something flared in me, then—a question that had been prickling beneath my skin like sea nettle spines.

"Why is it your people are not treated equally?" The words came unbidden, bitter on my tongue. "Why does the shape of one's body decide their worth? Man, woman. Why does it matter if a man chooses to mate with another man—"

His hand rose swiftly, a feather-light hush, but his gaze darted around us, sharpened by alarm.

"We can speak of this," he said lowly, "but not here. Not in the open."

"Why not here?" I pressed. "If it must be silenced, then surely that proves something is wrong."

He sighed, long and heavy, rubbing the bridge of his nose before pushing a hand through his hair—those rich brown locks now slightly disheveled by the gesture.

"Yes. Of course. You're right. It's only—some subjects, if overheard, can be twisted into accusations. Dangerous ones."

"Because of how I look?" My voice dropped. "How can appearance alone accuse?"

His jaw tensed. "Did someone say something to you?" he asked, eyes narrowing.

"No,"

A hush fell between us. Dust motes danced in the shafts of light pouring through high arched windows, golden and slow like time itself had softened in this space.

"I know Gadimore is far from perfect," Titus said at last. "But it has been worse. And it can—will—be better. I will see to that."

His voice quieted, but the conviction in it did not.

"Change, when it is built on cruelty, comes swiftly and with fire. But change that is meant to better—it takes longer. It requires patience, relentless voices, and the breaking of habits people have mistaken for truths."

I studied him in that moment—this prince born to power yet speaking as though he carried the weight of change in his hands. And perhaps he did.

Though part of me was annoyed—no, angered—by the quiet injustice of it. That someone born into this world should carry a heart seemingly untouched by its rot. And yet... another part of me, could not help but admire the shape of him.

Not his form, though even that would have tempted a lesser being. No—it was the conviction, that flickering ember of hope in him that refused to be dimmed. I feared it. Envied it. Hungered to understand it. My face warmed without permission. I turned away from his gaze, brushing my fingers against the book I'd pulled free, as if by adjusting it I might also put my composure back into place.

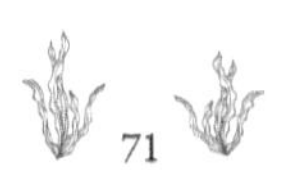

"Will you show me more of your chaos?" I asked, voice softer than before. Then, catching myself, "Your arcane, I mean."

"So you *were* waiting for me," he said, his voice touched with levity, gaze softening into something lighter—almost teasing.

"Your palace leaves much to be desired," I replied, dry as salt air. "I was in desperate need of amusement."

A smile curled at the corner of his mouth. "Mm. I see. You're aware, I presume, that I am a prince and not entertainment?"

I stepped closer, the distance between us thinning. My fingers lifted, just barely grazing the cool weight of his circlet. "The metal atop your head was a subtle clue... among other things."

"*Other things?*" His voice dipped into curiosity, head tilting with that ever-present gleam behind his eyes.

What *did* I mean? The tousled brown of his hair catching sunlight like threadbare silk, the gentle arrogance of his posture and broad shoulders, the warmth behind a smile too beautiful for my own comfort?

"The haughtiness that seems to plague human nobility," I answered coolly as I turned my back to him.

Behind me, the floor echoed beneath his boots. "You think I'm haughty?" he asked as he moved to walk beside me. "Do I truly strike you as such, or is this a jest?"

A smirk brushed my lips.

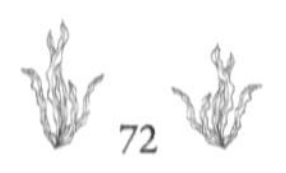

"I do try to be virtuous," he went on, half-defensive, half-laughing, "So if I have offended, I offer my sincerest—"

A laugh broke from me—quiet, unguarded. It escaped before I could recall it. He was not haughty. Far from it. But watching him fumble with the idea was, admittedly, charming.

"So it was a jest," he murmured, laughter stirring in his chest.

"Yes, Your Highness," I said, with all the human regality I could manage.

"On another note," he said, stepping suddenly into my path. I halted just short of him. "Your slight against my home did not go unnoticed, Rylen. Before I indulge your curiosity for the arcane, I intend to show you just how delightful confinement here can be."

"So you admit I'm confined to this cage of yours?"

"For your recovery," he returned evenly, "nothing more. Just until we understand what befell Captain LeVesque and the others aboard his vessel. Then you'll be permitted to return to the coastal garrison. Everything will return to its proper place."

He paused, watching me as if trying to peer past my skin and into the thoughts curling beneath. "Perhaps," he added, "we ought to revisit the shoreline—where you washed ashore. It may stir the memories you've misplaced."

There was nothing to be found but perhaps this was my answer to another matter, neatly placed like an offering at my feet. Go to the sea. Let the tide take him to Morvena. Let debts be paid by wave and whirlpool instead of my own hands. Let him vanish before I must choose what I already dread.

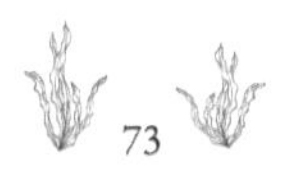

"Yes," I said, my voice a still surface. "Let us go now."

But he shook his head, his smile turning sly.

"Not yet," he said. "Let us wait until the sun is young again. Tomorrow. Tonight, you and I will explore the palace grounds. There is beauty here you've not yet seen."

"Is this your idea of beauty?" I asked dryly, lifting the hem of my sleeve to veil my nose. The air reeked of wet hay, damp wood, and the heavy scent of animals—thick and cloying in a way that clung to the back of one's throat.

Titus turned his head to glance at me from where he stood within the shadows of the stables, one hand stroking the length of a horse, the other beginning to fasten strips of leather along its spine. "The horses," he said, with a crooked smile, "are beautiful. The stables—not so much." A light laugh escaped him, warm and unguarded. "But no, this is only the means to the beauty, not the destination itself."

I stepped back as he led the creature forward, its hooves echoing against stone. "I thought you said we were not to leave the palace grounds."

"We aren't." He tilted his head as if I'd asked something foolish. "The palace grounds stretch across dozens of acres—gardens, meadows, forest paths. And past those, more acres. More walls."

He offered me the reins.

I blinked down at them. "I do not know how to direct a horse."

"You don't ride?" he asked gently, the way one might speak to someone confessing a strange absence in their education. But he didn't wait for my answer. His hands were already moving, unfastening the leather with practiced ease.

"We won't go far," he said. "And I'm a good rider. You'll only need to balance and hold on."

My body tensed, unbidden memories clawing their way up from beneath the surface—of my face smashed against iron of the guards attire, my limbs bruised and bent by the ceaseless rhythm of hooves beneath me, the unforgiving dig of the leather's ridges. Pain that clung to the bones. I swallowed against the nausea it summoned.

He smiled again, softer this time. "We'll need a different horse then," he murmured, taking back the reins with no trace of impatience.

He vanished into the stable's belly and returned moments later, leading another creature into the light.

She was immense. A dark, powerful shape with flecks of russet scattered like flame across her flanks. Her movements were graceful, but it was the kind of grace that came with danger—like a wave rearing back before it breaks.

"She's gentle," Titus said, catching the shift in my expression I hadn't meant to let show. "Brisa. She's used to bareback riding—she won't throw us. Slower, but smooth." He

draped linen over her back in place of the harsh leather, his movements gentle and slow.

Then, with a flick of his wrist, he reached for my hand. I stiffened, but he didn't let go. He guided my fingers to the creature's snout. Her skin was warm, velvet-soft. She exhaled, a heavy breath through her nostrils that stirred my hair.

"Brisa," Titus said gently, "this is Rylen."

I wasn't sure whether the noise she made was one of greeting or protest.

Titus released my hand, then hauled himself up with the ease of someone who belonged there. The horse shifted, metal ringing softly beneath her hooves. He extended his hand to me, palm open, waiting.

"Ready to be entertained?" he asked, a glimmer of mischief in his tone.

I reached for him. His hand closed around mine—warm, firm, unyielding—and he pulled me upward as though I weighed nothing. My chest pressed to his back as I found my seat atop the great beast, her body thrumming beneath us like a living tide.

I didn't answer his question.

But I held on.

Titus was right. There was beauty, more than I expected, the further we drifted from the palace. Stone gave way to soil, carved paths to wilder trails. The further we rode from marble walls and regimented rows of hedges, the more it all began to open—green stretching endlessly around us in soft waves, gentle and alive. It reminded me of the sea. So much

green overhead it should have overwhelmed me, and yet... it brought peace.

"Are you doing alright back there?" Titus' voice cut through the quiet. I felt the subtle shift of his back beneath me as he glanced over his shoulder. "We're almost there."

I pressed my face lightly to his back, to the fabric warmed by his skin. This ride was smoother than the last, slower—gentler. But still, there was something in the pit of my stomach that twisted. A tide shifting the wrong way. Though there was comfort in his frame. In the way he sat steady atop Brisa, unmoved by the wind or the world around us. In the way his hand would gently cuff my forearm when the trail suddenly bumped or curved. It was a silent tether that stirred something inside me. A yearning, a softness and a safety I hadn't known I craved.

"I feel... off."

"Please don't vomit on me," he said, voice strained with a half-laugh. "Or Brisa."

The horse's gait slowed to a rhythmic trot, then stilled completely.

"We can keep going," I murmured into the fabric of his tunic.

"We're nearly there anyway," he said. "But we'll need to go the rest on foot. Bit of climbing involved."

I pushed myself away from him and slid off the horse's back. The ground met me like an anchor—firm, solid, still. I inhaled deeply, willing the earth to quiet the roil in my stomach.

Titus led Brisa to a nearby tree and tied off her reins with ease, then stepped back toward me. From some pocket of his trousers, he withdrew a small leather pouch. He poured something into his palm—tiny seeds, dark and fragrant.

"Fennel," he said. "It helps with nausea. Not as strong as ginger, but I keep that for voyages at sea."

I stared at the seeds in his hand, dubious. "I'm to eat this?"

"Yes," he chuckled, lifting a brow. "Staring at it won't cure you."

My fingers brushed his palm as I took a few seeds, then brought them to my mouth.

The taste was... strange. Mild, yet sharp. Slightly sweet with an undertone that reminded me of crushed herbs left too long in the sun. It was not unpleasant, but it lingered—clingy and wild on the tongue.

I grimaced despite myself.

"Why the face?" Titus asked, grinning. "It barely tastes like anything."

Perhaps it's just me. I mused to myself. *Or this form. But everything tastes stronger. Sharper.*

Though merfolk didn't need to eat—our bodies sustained by the currents, nourished through gills as the sea filtered all we required—there were times of indulgence. Times of celebration that called for something more. On such occasions it was always something sweet: the tender fruits of underwater groves, the nectar of flowering kelp, and berries that shimmered like pearls. Up here, nothing had quite compared. The flavors were too loud, too layered.

"I find I do not like the taste of most things here." I said with a sigh.

Titus watched me for a moment, his smile softening. "Well then," he said lightly, slipping the pouch back into his coat, "I suppose I'll just have to find something you do like the taste of before you leave."

We trailed deeper into the forest, the canopy growing denser above us until it opened suddenly, spilling light onto a clearing.

"Okay," Titus said, stepping forward. "Stop and listen."

I obeyed, stilling my breath. At first, all I heard was wind. It whispered through brush and branches, rustling the leaves. Birds called softly from somewhere overhead, distant and safe in their nests.

But beneath it all... something else.

I knelt down, letting my fingers trail through the grass, cool and damp beneath my touch. I listened harder, closing my eyes. There—it was faint, but distinct. A trickle. Flowing. Water.

"You hear it?" Titus asked, a wide grin tugging at his lips.

I looked up at him, confused. He was practically brimming with excitement—over water. He was a sailor. If he missed the sea, why not simply go to it?

"I lied to you," he said suddenly, and I stood, instinct tensing. "Not entirely. Valtherion does grant magic, yes, but he

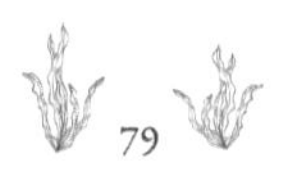

isn't the only way. Not many know that. I don't think many care to ask. They follow what they've been taught, what's easy."

He took a step toward the clearing's heart, his eyes scanning the trees. "But if you listen to the world around you... really listen... everything has arcane. I think there are more ways to learn it than anyone realizes. Even someone like you could, if you tried."

My brows furrowed. *Someone like me.* His words lit a slow burn in my mind. If I could learn this chaos—this human power—it could become my edge. My key to surviving, to escaping after my victory.

"Sorry," he added with a self-conscious laugh. "I know the ramblings of a madman might be—well. Let me show you."

He dropped to his knees, fingers threading through the grass. "Everything sings a song. The wind, the roots, the water. You just have to learn how to hear it. And once you do, it's not enough to recognize the notes. You have to sing them back. Every pitch, every tone. If you can match their song..."

He glanced up, his voice lowering into reverence. "You can do unspeakable things."

The ground beneath us trembled—subtle at first, then growing stronger. I stepped back instinctively.

"I was hunting deer when I heard the water below," he continued. "I wanted to reach it, so I sat here. And then I heard another sound... the earth."

Shapes began to form in the dirt around his hand as it pressed deeper into the grass—lines, symbols, familiar and

foreign, echoing the ones he'd drawn on my palm the night before.

Then he rose and moved beside me.

The ground gave way.

Collapsed inward in a slow, spiraling breath until a wide hole opened at our feet. The sound of water roared beneath us now—louder, clearer.

"Here comes the climbing part," Titus said, running a hand through his hair with a small, amused grin.

"You want us to descend into that?" My eyes widened as I looked between him and the hollow earth. "Wait—are we not going to acknowledge that you unraveled the land like cloth beneath your fingers?"

I reached out, grabbing his forearm as he stepped closer to the edge.

"Can all humans do this?"

He tilted his head, a flicker of a smile returning. "I'd like to think I'm an exceptional arcanist. But it wouldn't be very virtuous of me to say so outright, now would it?"

He was maddening.

And utterly fascinating.

But his display left me filled with questions, echoing through the quiet corridors of my mind. Who else in this court held such power? And more pressingly—what was the breadth of it?

"Can you show me how to do that?" I asked—my voice low, then softening, almost breaking. "Please, Titus."

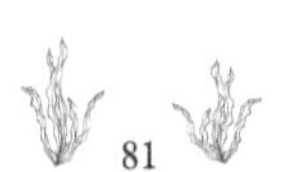

Something shifted in him at my plea. A flicker of warmth danced across his face. "I can try," he said, his voice stripped of any pretense, gentle as a promise. "But first... let me show you this."

He led the way, descending into the earth he had so effortlessly parted. His steps were careful, slow, and steady, the soles of his boots brushing loose dirt and crumbling stone. The narrow passage was tight, carved by chaos and conviction both, walls pressed in with the damp scent of soil and root.

I followed, though my limbs—still new—betrayed me. The incline was steeper than it seemed, and the clumsy precision of these legs wavered under me. My footing slipped. I cursed under breath—too late to catch myself—only to feel his hands at my waist, steadying me with quiet ease.

"You have me," he murmured, and I hated how the words anchored something in me. *Hate.* It wasn't hate. It was guilt—quiet, persistent, and utterly misplaced. A feeling I had no right to carry, yet couldn't set down.

He took my hand then—his fingers warm, calloused, grounding. We moved deeper. The tunnel opened wider ahead, unnaturally smoothed, carved with intention. It was not time that had shaped this place—it was him.

"How many times have you come here?" I asked, voice hushed, as though afraid to wake something sleeping in the dark.

"Too many to count," he said with a soft laugh. "But you are the first to follow."

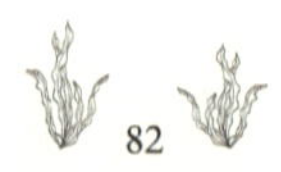

The words fluttered against my chest, delicate and damning. Why did they affect me so? Why did I care?

I cleared my throat, seeking to chase the fluttering thing away. "Were you not afraid? It must have been unknown... You could have been buried alive. Or found something waiting for you."

"I suppose I should have been," he admitted, tilting his head. "But I've always let curiosity guide my hand. I act first, then reflect—though I've been told that's a flaw."

With a flick of his wrist, fire bloomed. It curled into being without smoke, a small miracle resting in his palm. The light painted the tunnel in golds and ochres, throwing his features into soft relief—the curve of his cheek, the focus in his brow, the glint of something restless in his eyes.

"I've always been like this. With my arcane, too. Always wondering how far it can go... what lies just beyond the known." He looked ahead, but his voice seemed to speak inward. "Arcane is meant to be reserved—strictly bound to service, to structure. That's what they teach. But I don't believe that's all it is. I don't think we're meant to wait for permission to hear the world speak to us. You only need to listen."

He turned to me then, and in that moment he was not just a prince—not just human. He was something else entirely. Wild in his curiosity, reverent in his wonder. A man who had once knelt in a field and asked the ground to sing.

Strange, I thought. *What a strange, foolish, beautiful man.*

"What is that?" I breathed, the words barely a tremor against the soft rush of water. Ahead, a faint blue glow spilled

through the mouth of a narrow opening—like moonlight breaking through the ribs of the earth.

"That," Titus said, his voice gentle, almost boyish with wonder, "is what I wanted to show you."

With a simple flick of his wrist, the fire he'd conjured vanished, swallowed by the damp darkness. His face, now lit only by the otherworldly blue beyond, was smiling—wide and unguarded—as he stepped forward, his figure brushing against the crystalline shadows.

I followed.

The passage gave way to a cavern vast and echoing, carved by time and water into something that felt holy. A subterranean spring lay before us, water slipping from one edge to the other before vanishing beneath a submerged tunnel, as though the earth itself drank it in.

Above, the ceiling shimmered like a captured sky. Glowworms clung to the jagged teeth of the cavern roof—stalactites bathed in indigo light. Crystals embedded in the stone walls caught the glow and multiplied it, painting the air with fractured stars. It was a galaxy buried in stone.

Titus turned to me, his voice hushed. "That's what I was trying to mimic last night... but I fear I gave you stars instead." He rubbed the back of his neck, sheepish but hopeful. "Well? What do you think?"

I crossed my arms, not from cold but from the strange ache in my chest. "It's beautiful," I said, gaze never leaving the ceiling. And it was—achingly so. It reminded me of home. Of the grottos far below the ocean's skin, where phosphorescent algae clung to stones like lullabies waiting to be sung.

"There is beauty everywhere," Titus murmured beside me. "You just need to know where to look."

There it was again—that flicker of awe. The same expression I had seen before, long ago, when we were boys. I wished he remembered me. Truly, I did.

But a part of me was relieved he didn't.

Because if he remembered—if those memories came rushing back—then what I had come here to do would become unbearable.

My boots pressed against scattered stone as I stepped closer to the water's edge. I dipped my fingers into the surface. The stream kissed my skin, soft and cool. It was not the sea. But it was something close. Close enough to ache.

"Can you swim?" Titus asked, his voice light, playful.

"Of course," I replied before thinking, the words like muscle memory. But the truth unsettled me. I no longer moved within the body that had danced with the tide since birth. This form—borrowed, reshaped—was not meant for salt or current. Could I still move through water as I once did?

"Then shall we?" he asked.

I turned just in time to see him undoing the leather at his hips, laying his sword with deliberate care upon the cave floor. His hands lifted his shirt and drew it over his head. The fabric fell, and so did my gaze.

The light caught the defined play of muscle across his abdomen, the trail of dark hair that meandered downward and

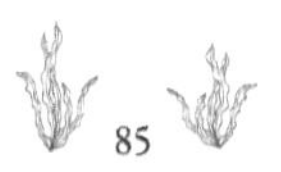

vanished beneath the waistband of his trousers. Merfolk bore no hair but on their heads, and I was caught in the strange, forbidden curiosity of how far his traveled.

As if summoned by thought alone, his fingers moved again—this time to his trousers, easing them just low enough to expose the sharp line of his hips.

Then he paused.

I looked up—and found his eyes already on me.

Caught.

His flush bloomed like a petal unfurling, sudden and unguarded. He froze in place, half undressed, half disarmed, like a myth caught between truths.

My face burned with the heat of my own gaze. Had I stared too long? Was it shameful here, to look so openly?

"I—I'm sorry, I didn't mean..." My voice faltered as I looked away, stranded between apology and admission.

"No, it's alright. I'm not usually shy. I just..."

The rest was swallowed by the sound of water parting as he plunged into it. The glow of the cavern caught on his skin as he waded deeper, the ripples folding around him. "Will you join me?" he asked, his voice echoing gently off the walls as he drifted back with slow strokes, leaving a shimmer in his wake.

"I confess, I cannot quite recall whether I know how to swim. So please, Your Highness, do be prepared to rescue me if I begin to drown." I said it with a faint smile, hoping levity might scatter the weight that hung unspoken between us.

Titus arched a brow, his lips curving in wry amusement. "Entertain you, instruct you, and now save you?

Truly, your expectations of me know no bounds." His gaze lifted—purposefully, perhaps—skimming past me as I began to unfasten my outer layers.

A question lingered unspoken between us. If it were improper to look, why did he disrobe before me so easily? And if I was not to watch, why did he feel so much like an invitation?

I dipped my foot in first, the chill licking up my leg, before easing my body into the spring, fingers clinging to the stone ledge. I felt heavier somehow, though I knew I weighed less in this form. This was not the sea, yet it was still water—I could bend it to my will, coax it to hold me. But would he feel it? Would he know?

I turned to him. "Titus."

He was at my side in an instant, as though I had called him with more than words. "Right. Of course—you're unsure if you—perhaps best to stay near the shallows—"

But I let go.

The world blurred as I sank. My limbs moved instinctively, yet gracelessly, flailing instead of flowing. The water pressed in, indifferent, unforgiving. I opened my mouth to breathe and drew in nothing but cold.

Panic swelled in my chest, sharp and consuming. Then I felt the pressure of arms around me, then a pull and I was rushed upward.

We broke the surface together, and I gasped, coughing, clawing weakly for breath. My hands found his shoulders, clinging.

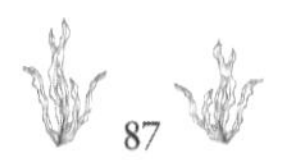

He held me fast—one arm secured around my waist, the other gripping the ledge to anchor us both. His body was warm against mine, steady.

"Are you alright?"

"That was foolish of me," I said softly, each word catching in my throat like seaweed in a net.

"Just a touch," he said, a quiet laugh beneath his breath.

I looked up at him—and he at me.

His hand lifted, brushing a wet strand of hair from my face with a tenderness that undid me. The world stilled. There was only the hush of the water and the erratic thrum of my heart, loud and tremulous in my ears.

Slowly, hesitantly, I leaned in. My lips ghosted his, a breath between us, and then I closed the distance. He didn't retreat or pull away—instead, he pressed against mine, steady and sure, as if this was what he had been waiting for. And for a moment it was just us. Forbidden. Desperate. My lips against his.

"Rylen," he whispered against my mouth. I froze.

"I'm sorry," I breathed. "I shouldn't have—"

But I was a creature of longing. Merfolk always were. There is always something that calls to us, something that gleams just beneath the surface, waiting to be touched. I knew, with a sick sort of clarity, that Titus was mine.

I tried to pull back. My palms pressed against his chest, my body half slipping again beneath the surface. But he caught me once more, our bodies crashing together in a tangle of limbs and heat.

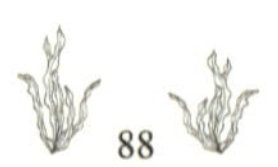

"Rylen," he said again, voice low. "It's alright. You needn't apologise. I just... I fear you may be mistaken in your reading of me. I don't—" he hesitated, swallowed—"I don't fancy men."

But then his gaze faltered, dropping to my mouth, along with his conviction.

He kissed me.

Soft at first, unsure. Then again. Again. Our lips parted only to find each other once more, hungrier each time. His hand cupped my jaw, and I melted into him, lost to the fire behind my ribs and the chill of the water.

His hips moved gently against mine, a slow, tentative press that stirred a strange, electric pleasure between us. A low sound slipped from me—half gasp, half sigh—unbidden, unfamiliar. A hardness pressed against me and I pulled back just enough to glance downward. Beneath its glimmering surface, I caught a fleeting glimpse—both our bodies stirred, aroused, hard. The friction felt good—impossibly—good. And so we continued to press against each other.

I had never known this before. For merfolk, such a reaction was sacred, stirred only by the pull to bond, to mate. Was that what this was? Did I want to offer myself to Titus as one would to a life-pair? Did he want me the same?

"I—I'm sorry," he stammered, his voice barely above the soft lap of water as his movements came to a halt. "I've never... I've never kissed anyone. I've never done any of this."

"I haven't either," I whispered, the heat blooming once again in my cheeks.

Among my kind, mating was for life. And I had never yearned for it—never had the time or the desire. Not until now. The thought was dangerous, absurd even. Titus was human. A human whose heart I had promised to deliver to Morvena.

"For what it's worth…" he hesitated, gaze searching mine, "I do like men. But considering how things are, this—*we*—must remain secret, Rylen. I hope you understand."

"I do," I said. "This won't go any further. It can't."

"Why not?"

"I think you know." I looked away, hoping the ambiguity might spare me from voicing the real truth. If this continued, I would crave more. I would want more of something I cannot have. I would lose myself in the way he felt against me, in the way his breath faltered and heart stuttered. I cannot, will not allow myself to be bound to a human.

Silence fell, thick and fraught. Then softly, achingly so—"Can we pretend?" he asked. "Just for a moment. That none of it is forbidden. That the world is kind."

His words hit like a tide. I looked at him—dripping wet, hair clinging to his skin, the faint glow of the cavern's light reflecting in those green eyes—and I found I had no strength to deny him. No will to deny myself.

I said nothing. I simply commanded the water rise beneath us, gently lifting our bodies until he was pressed against the cold stone ledge. My lips found his, desperate and deep. His hands slid to my waist, then lower, pausing at the curve of my backside before drawing me closer with quiet urgency. Our hips moved, the friction slow at first, desire

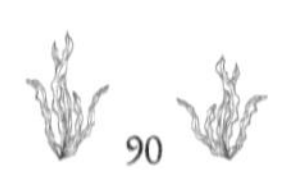

building as our bodies met in rhythm. Our breaths tangled, and the water around us trembled—charged with the heat of what we dared to feel, if only for this one, stolen moment.

"I—I want to try something," he murmured against my lips, his voice trembling with intent. One hand slipped between us, steady and sure, until his fingers wrapped around both of us—his palm warm, his grasp unpracticed but eager. "If it's too much, tell me. I'll stop."

His touch firmed, drawing us together—our shafts aligned, flushed and aching, as he began to move his hand in a rhythm that stole the breath from my lungs.

"Tides..." The word tore from me, guttural and raw, my forehead collapsing to the curve of his shoulder. My arms caged around him, hands finding the ledge behind, desperate for something to anchor me.

"Does it... feel good?" His voice was a gasp, his breath fanning over my ear.

"Don't stop," I whispered—no, begged. There was no dignity in it, only the terrible beauty of want.

"I won't," he promised, and pressed his lips to my temple.

The tension inside me coiled, unbearably tight, pressure building in waves that left me trembling. My fingers dug into the stone, aching with restraint, but it was all too much—his hand, the heat, the slick, silken friction. My lips brushed the curve of his neck, then my teeth followed, grazing gently before I sank them in.

"R-Rylen," the sound spilled from his throat—a sharp, breathless whimper that broke against my skin—and it shattered me.

A trembling exhale tore from my throat as the pressure within me reached its breaking point. It was like being caught in a riptide—pulled under by something vast and consuming. My muscles tensed, a shudder wracking through me as my senses narrowed to the pull of Titus' hand, the slick heat of our bodies, the soft breath of his voice near my ear. And then—release. A surge of pleasure so sharp it bordered on pain, stealing my breath. The world vanished and I unraveled completely in his grasp.

His grip on me loosened, then fell away entirely. Gentle hands slid to my hips, guiding a measure of distance between us as the hush of water ebbed around our bodies.

"I didn't mean for us to make such a mess," he said with a sheepish smile, though his voice was still low, breathless.

Milky ribbons drifted between us, clinging faintly to his skin before being carried away by the spring's slow current.

My gaze lowered to his neck. There, beneath the shimmer of glowlight, a bruise bloomed—violet, deep and tender, unmistakably the shape of my teeth. I reached for it instinctively, fingers trembling as they brushed against the mark. "Titus... I'm sorry. I didn't mean to hurt you."

Shame swelled in me like a tide. I had always been warned that one could lose control in the throes of mating, but I thought I had kept myself contained. This hadn't truly been that—I hadn't released inside him. I had not been *inside* him.

And besides, he was a man. A human man. I couldn't breed him... but the instincts within me, primal and ancient, had whispered otherwise.

"You didn't hurt me," he murmured with a quiet laugh, eyes soft. "It felt... good."

"You liked it?" I asked, uncertain.

"I did," he said, and reached to cup my cheek with a hand that trembled, just slightly. "And you? Did it feel right to you?"

I looked at him—at the glowworms mirrored in his eyes, at the gentleness threaded through his expression. "I've never known anything more desirable," I said honestly. "Or more consuming than this."

Than him.

Chapter Five

"Everything sings a song." Titus' words from earlier echoed in my mind. I understood them now. The sea had always spoken to us, and in that connection, it granted us magic. We called, and it answered.

My gaze shifted to the candle flickering on my bedside table. Its flame danced to the rhythm of the cool breeze drifting in through the window. His theory was that anyone could access chaos—if only they listened.

So I tried. I closed my eyes and listened. And listened. And listened.

Nothing.

Only the distant clink of armor as the guards paced outside, the hushed murmur of servants moving across the grounds as they readied the palace for nightfall.

But if I could learn this, and then if I could hear the song of the earth—I might be able to reach that spring again.

Trade these legs for my tail. Just for a little while. Even escape the palace grounds unnoticed to the sea. I would return before dawn. I simply... I was restless. The bed, though soft, could never compare to the embrace of the sea.

Though there was another embrace that came close. Titus.

My mind drifted to earlier. The warmth of his body pressed against mine. The whisper of his breath against my neck. The way his lips tasted. My fingers traced from my lips down, lingering at the familiar ache blooming below.

They slipped beneath the waistband of my trousers, brushing against the hardness there. It pulsed, straining. My hand mimicked his movements from earlier—slow, deliberate.

My eyes fluttered shut and I heard his voice again—those soft, eager sounds he'd made, so close to my ear. My back arched, breath hitching.

What has this human done to me?

This was not our way. We did not pleasure ourselves. We mated to breed. And yet... there was something about him.

"Titus," I moaned, my voice breathless as my release came in warm waves, my length twitching in my grip.

My hand slowed, eventually falling still. "Titus," I whispered again. A quiet plea. A yearning I could not deny.

"Rylen," a familiar voice purred from the darkness.

A searing heat bloomed in my chest, burning against the cold that surrounded me. I couldn't move, couldn't see—only feel the pain radiating through me.

"Do not forget yourself. You must make it all crumble, Rylen. Bring them to their knees. Every one of them, for the sake of Aserian. It is your duty," Morvena said, her voice a caress dripped in command.

"Rylen."

Another voice shattered the void.

Elisienne stood at my bedside, her hand resting gently on my shoulder, brows furrowed with concern. "I apologize for the intrusion," she said softly. "I knocked, but you did not answer. You did not stir when I entered or called your name."

Her hand withdrew slowly as I reached toward the heat at my chest. My fingers brushed the talisman—hot to the touch. The skin beneath it throbbed, tender and sore.

Her eyes widened as she caught sight of the burn beneath my open shirt. "Sir, your flesh—it's red. Should I send for Lord de Clairvaux?"

She turned to go.

"No." I rose swiftly, catching her forearm. "It's nothing. I'm fine."

By the sea, I didn't want that lunatic anywhere near me.

"Yes, sir," she murmured, dipping her head. "I-I was sent to ready you. You are to depart with His Majesty this morning."

Right—the visit to the sea. The plan had been to see if it might jog my memories of the fleet. It wouldn't. But I had agreed to humor the notion... to get Titus into the water. To command it to carry him to Morvena.

That thought now made my stomach turn and my heart ache.

"Shall I give you a moment?" Elisienne asked carefully.

"No, no. I'm fine," I said, standing fully.

What followed felt like a mockery of routine. A simulation of what I assumed mornings looked like for those with no true place in the upper echelons of human court. Elisienne bathed and dressed me despite my resistance. I was made to drink that awful tea again. The food had flavor this time, yes—but none of it settled right.

Through it all, I waited. Waited for the moment I would see Titus again. My thoughts clung to him, circling back to Morvena's voice. Her words hadn't been just a reminder of duty. They were a warning.

A threat.

"Ah, Rylen. Are you ready?" Titus greeted me in the corridor, a warm smile on his face.

"I had no choice but to be," I said casually as he stepped beside me, his arms folding neatly behind his back.

"You smell sweet," he murmured, his voice dropping as he leaned in just slightly.

"Elisienne had me bathed this morning," I replied, attempting to swallow down the heat rushing to my face.

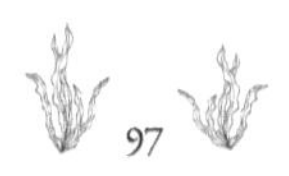

"I apologize if the staff comes across as overwhelming. It's merely their way—they don't know how else to tend to someone as demanding yet self-reliant as you... You are quite a handful. Parts of you anyway," he said lightly, the tease woven into the hush of his voice as we moved through the corridor. His posture remained perfectly poised, his gaze forward, every inch the picture of regal composure.

No one passing us would guess what he was truly saying. What a risky little game he played. How entertaining.

"And what of you?" I asked, matching his quiet tone, my own eyes fixed ahead. "Do you let their hands tend to you as freely, or do you prefer to manage things yourself? Tell me, Your Highness... do you prefer to *be in* command, or *to be* commanded?"

"I—" There was the slightest hitch in his breath—barely noticeable—before he composed himself. "I prefer to be in control," he said smoothly, then after a brief pause and a quick throat-clearing, added, "Though... for the right sort of assistance, I might allow myself to be guided."

This was dangerous. In more ways than one. For him, it was the fear of being caught with another man. For me, it was far more treacherous—making sure desire didn't drown out my duty.

And yet, it was already happening. I was unraveling.

"How virtuous of you," I murmured, my voice velveted with intent as my hand slipped beneath the waistband of Titus' trousers. My fingers wrapped around his length, hot and hard, as I pressed my body flush against his. The soft thud of his back hitting the stable wall sent a jolt of satisfaction through me.

We were hidden by the stacks of hay, the sounds of shifting hooves and rustling straw muffling the catch of our breath, the soft sounds slipping from parted lips.

"Hard to be virtuous when you're like a siren," he whispered, voice trembling, head tipping back. "You lure me into sin."

"You could always resist." My lips brushed the shell of his ear, teasing. "Surely your will is stronger than your perversion."

"I'll never resist you, Rylen," he said, breathless. His hand buried itself in my hair, drawing me into a kiss that burned—open-mouthed, desperate, tasting of need and surrender.

That aching pull clawed at my restraint, the feral instinct to take, to claim. My body throbbed with it. My breath came harsh against his skin as I turned him, hands splaying against the wall for balance.

I leaned in, burying my face between his shoulder blades as my hand reached around him, stroking his length with firm, eager care. My hips rocked gently against him, my arousal grinding into the curve of his backside.

I felt like a beast straining at its leash, unhinged. Though this was me holding back and I loathed it.

You cannot mate with him. You cannot bond. He is not yours.

His body shuddered, muscles tightening, and then came the sharp gasp and sudden twitch in my palm as he came—his release painting the wooden wall, the floor, all while he bit back a moan.

I forced myself to pull away, jaw clenched, trying to tame the ache in my groin.

"I... I didn't get to please you," he said hoarsely, head resting against his arm, breath still uneven. "Let me?" He turned to face me, already tucking himself back into his trousers.

"We have a long day ahead. I think my pleasure can wait," I said, forcing my voice to soften.

His mouth pulled into a pout, eyes locked on mine—by the sea, he was beautiful like this, still flushed and wanting.

"If it troubles you so deeply," I murmured, stepping closer, fingers brushing his collar to hide the bruise I'd left the night before, "then I'll allow you to make it up to me... another time."

"Swear to it?" he asked, voice husky, gaze heavy-lidded.

"A mer's—" I caught myself, quickly correcting, "I swear it."

There was a flicker of something in his expression, but then it faded into a warm smile.

"Perfect. Then shall we?" he said, and stepped past me into the light.

We stepped outside to find a large wooden vessel waiting for us—like the one Olivier had tethered to his horse, only far more regal. Intricate carvings adorned its frame, its

varnished finish catching the morning light. It didn't matter how lavish it appeared. I was simply grateful I wouldn't be forced onto another damned horse.

"We'll be taking a carriage," Titus said, his tone casual. "Harlowe's a ways off. This is easier for moving through the capital and to the smaller villages. Offers a bit of privacy."

One of the guards opened the half-door. Titus stepped in first. I followed, and it shut behind us with a soft clack of finality.

He settled on one side, sitting on one of the plush benches; I took the other. Our eyes locked. Mischief behind those emerald beauties. Then, with practiced ease, he slid further down his seat, inching closer until his knee brushed mine—then lingered, pressing between my legs with deliberate intimacy.

"How exactly did you come to meet Olivier Fenais?"

"Found me stumbling after I came ashore," I replied, voice even.

His fingers toyed with the edge of the curtain covering the small window. Only a sliver of light filtered through the carriage.

"And then what?" he asked—his tone smooth, unbothered—while his hand slid up my thigh, slow and steady.

"I—then..." The words faltered as his fingertips traced over the fabric stretched taut across the growing bulge in my trousers.

"And then what, Rylen?" he repeated, voice so calm, so commanding it made my breath catch. He sounded like he did

when addressing his men—authoritative, unbothered. But it was all a ruse just in case the guards heard.

I grabbed his wrist, halting him. "His horse nearly trampled me," I said flatly. Then, with just enough pressure, I guided his hand to wrap around the ridge of my arousal, forcing him to squeeze.

His lips parted, but he didn't speak. Just shifted forward, leaned in until his mouth hovered just above mine—his breath warm and tempting.

"What happened after that?"

"He took me in," I said, fingers threading into his soft brown hair, guiding his throat to my mouth. "Fed me. Bathed me. Clothed me. Let me rest."

"Bathed you?"

I smiled against his skin, my voice a playful whisper. "Is that jealousy I hear?"

"N-No.." The denial slipped out breathless.

"He ran the bath. I bathed alone," I said, returning to a more even tone—before trailing a kiss along the curve of his throat. "I told you... this could wait."

"But I've been lured again," he murmured quietly, his hand grazing my throat before curling beneath my chin. He tilted my face toward his, forcing our eyes to meet. "How am I supposed to temper myself when just the sight of you stokes every fire inside me?"

Then the carriage jolted over a bump in the road, the sudden motion forcing him back, putting space between us.

"Seems even the earth thinks you should wait," I said with a low chuckle.

He settled into his seat again, though I could still feel the heat of him—his hunger lingering in the air like smoke, thick and intoxicating.

And tides, the hunger between my legs didn't fade either.

The sun beat down, warm against my shoulders as our boots met the soil of Harlowe. Townsfolk gathered, their voices low, their gazes cutting through the late morning haze—not for me, but for their prince. Some watched in awe. Others, with quiet scrutiny.

Titus offered them a practiced smile, the kind I've seen him reserve for court and his subjects. Then, without a glance back, he moved toward his men to speak with them—cool, composed, as if we hadn't spent an hour in a carriage torturing ourselves with half-finished touches and the gnawing ache of restraint.

The salt-heavy breeze off the nearby sea helped clear my thoughts. That—and the few feet of space now between us.

The ground rumbled under the weight of two horses dragging a wide wooden cart through the town square. The crowd scattered, some returning to their routines, though a few

lingered, curious. Their prince, flanked by members of his Coastal Guard, wasn't a common sight here it seems.

My eyes locked onto the cart as it passed. Barrels brimmed with fish, nets tangled around their fins like the remnants of some violent struggle. Scales glinted in the light. Dozens of lifeless eyes stared skyward. All of it—taken. Ripped from the sea with nothing given in return but filth and intrusion. They had food on land. They didn't need this.

"Rylen," Titus' voice cut into my thoughts. "My men have duties to attend to, but the shoreline's not far. We can walk from here."

I didn't look at him. My gaze lingered on the cart.

"Are you hungry?" he asked.

"I don't eat what lives."

"They're already dead," he said, a soft chuckle trailing behind the words—until he saw the look I gave him. "Apologies. That does explain why I was told you don't eat much. I thought you were just... very particular."

"Do humans have no limits to what they'll consume?" I asked, voice sharp, the bitterness leaking through. "Do you feel no shame in killing and eating when you have so much else? You have grain, fruit, livestock. Yet you plunder the ocean as if it's yours to take."

He stiffened, just slightly. That flicker in his gaze—the warm light he always carried—dimmed for a beat.

Then his arms crossed. "You are human, aren't you?"

He tilted his head, a single brow raised.

"You always say 'humans' like it's something separate from you."

"I—I am human."

"Then promise me that, Rylen." His voice was gentle, but the challenge underneath it was unmistakable.

"I don't have time for your games," I said, turning away. "Let's go."

"Ah, Ry," he called behind me, a smile threading through his tone before I saw it. "It's this way. Unless you're hoping to end up in the farmland. By all means—enjoy your trek."

"You're being haughty, Your Highness," I muttered as I stepped past him, now heading in the right direction.

Silence stretched between us as we made our way to the shoreline, retracing the same path I had once taken when I first came to land. The only sounds were the shifting of sand beneath our boots and the whisper of waves.

"I feel as though you're upset with me," Titus finally said, stepping in beside me, matching my pace. "Have I done something wrong?"

"It's not what you've done," I answered. "It's what you haven't."

His brow furrowed as his hand reached—then quickly retreated, his gaze flickering around in search of prying eyes, though the beach lay empty. "What is it I haven't done?"

"What else do your people take from the sea besides fish?"

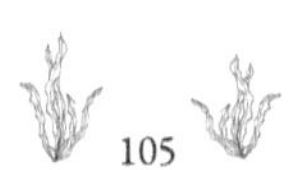

"Crustaceans. Oysters. Mussels. Obviously fish," he said, tentative. "Why?"

"Anything else?" My tone had sharpened.

He slowed. "I don't know what you're trying to make me say."

"What do you do to merfolk?" I stopped, turning to face him, my jaw tight.

He blinked. "Merfolk?"

"Yes. Merfolk. People of the sea. Cursed creatures of the waves—call them what you like."

"If you're asking whether we eat them, the answer is no. My father outlawed that the moment he took the throne."

King Beaumir outlawed it? My thoughts reeled. That didn't match what I knew—what I had *seen.*

I unraveled the scraped sail from around my waist and shoved it against his chest.

"Your king may have forbidden it," I snapped, "but why do your ships still trespass into our waters?"

He caught my wrists, holding my hands to his chest. "Rylen, what are you talking about?" His tone cracked with disbelief. "Gadimore's ships are under strict command, *my* command, not to disturb the mer. If they're being hunted, it isn't by our order—or it isn't known to us." His voice dipped, wounded. "Why do you hate Gadimore so much? You mock our customs at court, you speak of us like we're beneath you—and now this. You're not one of my men, are you?"

Before I could respond, the shift happened.

His movements were swift and deliberate. One twist and I was turned, my back pressing to his chest, arms folded tight across my torso. His breath brushed my ear—warm, steady, dangerous.

"Where is Captain Roland LeVesque?" he asked, voice low. "Where are my men?"

"I told you," I said, forcing my breath to stay calm, "they're dead."

"By your hands?" His grip cinched tighter around my waist. "I ask you again, Rylen, are you one of mine?"

"I am yours," I said, my voice unwavering, even as my heart thundered. I let myself relax against him. "I swear to you—I am yours."

It was the truth, in a way. Not the way he meant. But still the truth. Horrifyingly so.

His grip loosened. His chin came to rest on my shoulder. "I don't want to fight with you. I want this over. Please, Rylen... tell me what happened. So we can move past it."

I hesitated. "If I tell you, what then? Will you send me away? You said you remembered all your men—but you forgot me once. Will you forget me again, Titus?"

He didn't answer.

"I'm sorry this trip to the sea was a waste of your time and effort, Your Highness," I said, pulling from his hold. He let me go.

I walked toward the water. The scent of salt and sun hit me like a wall, the distant crashing of waves calling me back to

who I was. I stood at the edge, boots brushed by water, fighting to breathe through the weight in my chest.

What am I doing?

I was unraveling.

But if I told him the truth about his men—would this man, who looks at me with such light, such awe and want—would he see me as a monster? Would I be forced to flee back to the sea before I could even finish what I came here to do? And yet... what if he wasn't lying? What if it truly is forbidden in Gadimore? But no—no, I saw the flag. It was a Gadimore ship that dragged one of my own from the water as she screamed. It was a Gadimore ship I commanded the tides to swallow whole. I watched the ocean crush the hull, watched the men drown beneath the weight of their own cruelty.

Humans are liars. Manipulators. Monsters.

And yet...

"Rylen," Titus said behind me, his voice low and softened. "Forgive me. I should not have accused you. The weight of this—my men, their families—they're all depending on me to uncover the truth."

Humans are monsters, but mine isn't.

Chapter Six

There was a longing between us—wordless and yet impossibly loud. It needed no name, no declarations exchanged. It lived in the spaces between glances, in the hush of held breath. But beneath that quiet yearning, a shadowed truth coiled: this thing between us could not last. Not in this world. Not with who we were destined to be.

"Prince Titus."

A servant's voice met us at the palace doors, drawing us back into the gilded corridors of duty. He bowed low, eyes lifting only when summoned by silence. "His Majesty King Evren has returned early from Balthvidae. He brings with him a guest from their court and requests your presence. You are expected to be made presentable and punctual."

Titus exhaled, a breath too soft for the servant to notice, but I caught it. "Sooner than expected," he muttered, voice low enough to drown in. Then, turning to me, something

gentled in his expression—though his hand found the hilt of his sword, fingers curling as if bracing himself. "Rylen," he said. "You are free to do as you please. I will see you tonight. For confessional."

He left with the servant, posture sharpened by tension, leaving behind the echo of his voice and the absence of his warmth. I remained behind in the marbled stillness of the hall—half dreadful, half relieved by the servant's words.

The king had returned. And with him, my moment.

I could feel the talisman pressing warmer against my skin. Its edges had begun to sharpen again, slowly returning to its former state. I needed to leave. I needed to speak to Morvena.

My hand raised, beckoning a passing servant. "Send for Elisienne. Tell her I require a bath drawn in my chambers."

When the servant departed, I pressed my back to the cool stone of the corridor wall, grounding myself. My fingers drifted into my pocket, closing around the shell I'd taken from the Harlowe shore. I let my thumb pass over its spiraling form again and again, as if it might summon something—courage, conviction, absolution, something.

By the time I returned to my chambers, steam had begun to rise from the tub. The scent of oils lingered in the air—lavender, clove, the faintest trace of myrrh. A veil of warmth pressed against my senses.

This will work. It must. If the sea had not forsaken me, then it would answer.

Elisienne approached, her hands folded neatly at her waist, she offered a gentle incline of her head. "Shall I assist you in undressing, sir?"

"No," I replied, too quickly, then softened. "Thank you. I will bathe alone. Mathis suggested a long soak. He says I should be left to soak with my thoughts."

A lie, told too easily. A necessary one.

She nodded, her expression unreadable but respectful. "As you wish. Send for me when you have need of me."

She left quietly, shutting the door behind her. I waited, counting heartbeats, until her footsteps faded down the corridor. Then I moved—testing the weight of the furniture in the room, settling on a carved dresser of dark wood. The legs scraped softly against the stone floor as I eased it across, barring the door.

I stripped without ceremony, clothing folding to the floor like the shedding of skin. Slowly I sank into the water. It kissed my chest, climbed my throat. In one hand, I cradled the shell; in the other, I clutched the sea-glass talisman. "By the seas," I whispered, the words nearly lost to steam and trembling breath, "numb the pain that is to come."

I drew the talisman from around my neck and closed my eyes, pressing my back to the wooden wall of the tub, the wood groaning faintly beneath me. The stillness before the shift was always the worst—silence like a held breath before the scream.

It began as it did last time: a flush of warmth blooming in my veins, deceptively gentle, like the kiss of morning tide. And then the agony bloomed.

Heat surged through me, splintering into every nerve as bones bent and reformed beneath skin. I gripped the rim of the tub until my knuckles paled, until my fingers trembled with the effort of not crying out. My skin pulled taut, stretched over shifting muscle, and then tore in flashes as opalescent blue scales erupted. My breath turned ragged. I pressed my forehead to the wood, and the water shuddered with me as my tail unfurled into being.

Then came the part I feared most.

My throat began to close, the air turning thin—an intruder I could no longer accept. It scratched at my lungs, foreign and dry. I slipped beneath the surface, surrendering to the water's hold, and opened my mouth. The rush of it filled me, and for one breathless moment, I thought I would drown.

But then—

Change.

My lungs twisted. My heart slowed. Gills split open along my neck like blooming wounds, and I could breathe again. Truly breathe. My organs settled into their old rhythm, tide-bound and aching, and I realized just how long I had gone without this—how I had starved without knowing it.

I opened my eyes beneath the water, and everything stilled.

But it was wrong.

This water—it was not of the sea. It bore no salt-song, no pulse of tide. It would suffice, for now. But no mer could live long within it.

I reached through the water, searching for the shell I had let fall. Though the sea had not heeded my plea to ease the pain, I prayed it would stretch its grace far enough to grant me this: the magic to do what must come next.

I emerged from the water, my head tilting back as I drank in the brittle air of the land once more. We could breathe it, yes, but not for long. We needed the sea within us.

My tail drifted further into the bath's warmth as I shifted upright, spine pressing against the wooden tub's back, the weight of it grounding me. In my hands, I held the shell. I ran my fingers along its grooves, tracing the ridges like a map home. In the sea, it would have been enough. Just a shard of something true, and the waters come to me, ferrying me to its origin. But here, so far from salt and current, would the sea still listen?

A sharp thought cut through the haze: *I will need a way back.* And then I remembered—the spring. I had taken a pebble from its edge.

With effort, I leaned over the tub's rim, lifting myself just enough to reach for the pile of clothes. My hands fumbled through fabric and baubles, the collection of oddities I had gathered since arriving in Gadimore. Trinkets with no purpose.

"Like a Fiddler Crab, always hoarding," Coralie's voice rang in my mind, teasing. *"Though the crab needs it, you don't."*

Her laughter, light and unbothered, echoed in the space behind my eyes.

A breath caught in my throat. I missed her. I missed them all—my kin, my home, the hush of the deep and the pulse of our sacred currents. But if I found them now, would they allow me to leave to complete what needed to be done?

I sank once more into the water, the shell now pressed to my chest. My eyes slipped shut. I did not speak, not aloud. I called inward, to the ancient thing that lived beneath the waves. I called to the sea as I once had as a child, lost in the kelp forests.

There was silence at first.

And then—

A hum. Faint. A note struck in the deep.

The pull came slowly, like a tide crawling up the sand. The water around me shifted, responding. The air thickened, charged with salt. The bath darkened, rippled—and I whispered, "Take me home, I beg you."

A cold struck, fierce and biting as I was pulled. Submerged. Then came the warmth—familiar, sacred, cradling. The weight of water that knew my name. My body knew before my mind did: Aserian. Home.

A glimmer stirred in the waters ahead—silver flashes catching the fractured light. A school of aether herring swept in to greet me, their scales iridescent with shades of pearl and pale violet, like moonlight dancing over glass. Their long, ribbon-like fins trailed behind them like delicate silk banners, and as they spiraled around me in a slow, reverent vortex, I felt

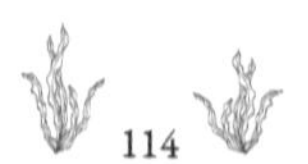

it—their joy, their wonder. It pulsed through the water like a song. My lips curled into a smile.

The shoal parted, though many lingered at the edges, unwilling to fully leave. From behind them, something immense approached, slow and sure as a drifting island. A gentle beast, a whale shark. Her hide shimmered with barnacled blues and quiet constellations, her great body gliding through the sea like a hymn made flesh. I reached out, fingers brushing the cool, rough velvet of her skin as she passed.

Oh, how I had missed home. The sea folded around me like a long-forgotten lullaby, salt and memory laced into every current. But even here, in the cradle of my birthright, joy did not fully take root. There was a thread of me still stretched taut above the waves—an ache that lingered. A part of me remained on land, restless and yearning, drawn to the warmth of a smile too gentle to forget, and eyes the color of spring leaves after rain.

"*Rylen.*" The voice did not travel through water. It moved deeper—slipping into my mind. It was Morvena.

With a soft touch in parting, I pushed away, my tail curling behind me as I descended toward the abyssal veil.

Below, the water dimmed to a hushed blue, and then blackened into ink. Life thinned. Shapes fled. At the edge of the chasm, lanternfish clustered, their bellies alight with flickering hues, offering one last gasp of light before the sea became unknowable.

I said nothing. I didn't need to. One followed.

Past the threshold, the currents shifted. Denser. Colder. Alive with intent. A quiet resistance pressed against my limbs—a warning woven into the very water: do not go farther. It was the sea's way of protecting its children from what dwelled beyond. But like before, I braced myself against the pressure and swam on, ignoring its whispered plea to turn back.

"You've returned," she purred, her voice curling through the waters, brushing against my skin though I saw no sign of her form. "You reek of chaos... but I do not sense what I asked for. Where is the heart, Rylen?"

A chill ran along my spine. Her tone was velvet over glass, soft but sharp. I swallowed hard, my gaze cutting through the gloom. The bioluminescent glow of her ruined palace had dimmed to a pulse, and even the lanternfish seemed to flicker uneasily. I could feel her power coiling through the water, thick and expectant.

"Or," she murmured, "have you come to offer me your own, dear prince?"

"No, I—" I faltered. *Why am I here?* I had a task, a plan. The moment to strike was close, so why was I here? I swallowed before speaking once more. "Chaos festers in human bloodlines. It runs through the Beaumir line. What if I gave you Evren instead?"

"King Evren?" Her laughter was a ripple, too slow, too knowing. Then she emerged, eyes like twin violets caught in a dying sunbeam, mouth curled in amusement as she drifted closer. "The bargain was for a prince's heart. Titus'. Did you think me so easily swayed?"

"But..."

She tilted her head, the sharp grace of her movement both predatory and poised. Her smile softened—dangerously so—as she circled me. "You love a human," she said, almost tenderly.

My eyes met hers before I could stop myself.

"The Prince of Gadimore, no less," she mused, her voice lilting with disdain and amusement. "What would dear Mother and Father say? Their only son, not climbing to land to save his people, but to kneel at the side of their enemy."

I felt my jaw tighten, heat coiling behind my ribs. "You're wrong. Gadimore is not our enemy. Titus told me—they're forbidden to hunt us."

Morvena's smile snapped. "I am never wrong, Rylen." Her voice cracked like a whip through water. "You saw the ship. You saw what they did. Have your human friends not already confessed that it was theirs?"

I said nothing. And in silence, I condemned myself.

She came closer again, drifting until her hands settled, cold and weightless, on my shoulders. Her voice dropped to a whisper at my ear.

"You know you cannot be with him. Not when he is unknowing of what you truly are. Not when you don't belong in his world." Her breath was a phantom against my skin. "Besides, the land is cruel. They do not suffer love between

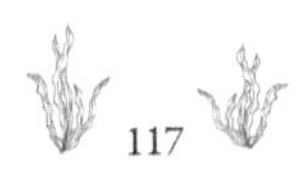

men. Not in Gadimore. Not in Lopharius. You will ruin him. They'll strip him of crown, of honor... perhaps even life."

She moved beside me, her hands trailing away.

"The land rots, Rylen. And that rot seeps into the sea. You would do well to carve it out while you can. Give me the prince. Or the sea shall bring me what is owed." Her voice cooled, final as stone. "Your people are better off with you alive."

Then she was gone, vanishing into shadow, and I was left to the silence—and the weight of the choice she had placed in my hands.

Her words rang clear, each syllable an anchor dropping into the pit of my soul. She didn't care whether King Evren lived or died—his life was a mere breath in the gale. What she hungered for was the chaos inside Titus. And if I could not deliver him to her hands, then she would take me as recompense. My life for my failure.

I had already betrayed my nature in more ways than I could count. The first was violence—unnatural to us, the last resort of creatures born of current and calm. The second was stepping onto land and shedding the sea's embrace.

We were not bred for war. Merfolk do not draw blood unless blood is drawn first. That was why Morvena had been cast into the abyss. She had not defended—she had lured, provoked, hunted. My father, ever devoted to the will of the waters, believed that if the sea wished to banish the humans, it would rise up and do so. But it hadn't. The waves still cradled their ships, still sang to their shores. *We* were the ones who drew too close to the surface, who forgot our place beneath the

blue. He had warned us—warned me—that safety lies in the deep. That the open sea, while ours by right, would never offer sanctuary if we danced too near the land.

But I had not listened. And in that recklessness, I had broken a final, unspoken law. I had given my affections to a human, I had given my heart to Titus.

My fingers curled tight around the stone from the spring as I began to ascend, the sea parting around me, stirred by my call before I'd even breached the veil of darkness. But just as the light began to return—just as the pull of the water began to give way—his voice reached me.

"Rylen."

My father.

Soft and sudden, carried like a current through silt and silence. But before he could speak again—before I could even turn toward it—I was gone. The abyss fell away and I broke through the familiar waters of Titus' hidden spring, far below the palace grounds. The dark chill of the deep replaced by warmth and glow.

My arms folded upon the stone ledge, head bowing with the weight of guilt and aching love. "Forgive me, father," I whispered into the saltless hush, my tail slipping through the water with a slow, resigned sweep.

My gaze lifted toward the sealed tunnel, the stonework and earth pressed tight. I let out a soft sigh. *Of course*—Titus had closed it when we left.

If ever there were a time to learn how to listen for chaos, it was now.

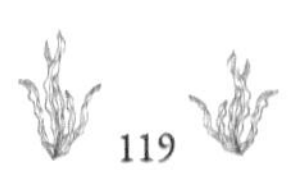

With trembling fingers, I slipped the talisman back over my neck. Then pressed my brow to my arm, bracing my hands against the stone's edge. The pain bloomed before the change—sharp and familiar, a pulling of bone and breath, sinew and skin. My body shuddered, twisted, until legs returned where tail had been.

I pulled myself from the spring, legs unsteady beneath me, water cascading from my frame in streams. I moved slowly, unsure of the ground beneath my feet, following the passageway deeper into darkness, further from the water. My fingertips brushed along the rough walls—dirt and stone, coarse with age—as I sought the sealed end.

Titus had told me he sat above once, in silence. That he listened, and so I would listen too.

I lowered myself to the earth, the cold seeping through my skin. My eyes closed as I allowed the darkness to fold over me. At first, there was only the echo of water, the familiar rhythm of droplets meeting stone.

Time slipped, and my mind drifted. Weariness crept over me. I was near sleep when it came—subtle as a whisper beneath the tide.

The first note.

It was not the water. No, this sound came from deeper still—from the marrow of the earth. The sea is fluid, ever-changing, a song of longing and return. But the ground... the ground held a different voice. Its music was slow and ancient, forged in silence and pressure, a song of stillness and waiting. It did not beckon. It endured.

And in its endurance, I listened. Truly listened—to every note, every cadence, every subtle tone. And then, I called back.

The dirt above me shivered. The ground shifted, vibrations humming through stone and soil. Tiny specks crumbled loose dusting my bare skin. I stood, hand reaching as I called louder, my mind a plea: *Let me back into the light.*

And the earth obeyed.

It parted just enough. A rough, uneven gap broke open above me. Sunlight spilled through in golden beams, warm and blinding. I squinted, shielding my eyes. It wasn't as seamless or refined as Titus' work, but it was enough. Enough to pass.

As the light touched my skin, realization sank in: I was exposed. Naked, dirt-smudged, and strange. The humans would think I'd gone mad again.

Perhaps, I thought, *this will serve me.* If I could convince them that the madness had worsened—twisted deeper into delusion—they might let me see the king. Might let me close.

"Rylen! What happened to you?" Elisienne's voice struck first. She rushed to me as I stepped into the palace's entrance hall, linen already in hand. She wrapped it around me with the care of a mother cradling her sick child.

The guards had summoned her and Mathis the moment I was spotted walking toward the palace—filthy and nude.

"Say, boy, what's come over you?" Mathis tutted, already directing a servant. "Have you not been drinking your

tea? Perhaps we should prepare a new one. Something stronger."

I didn't need to say a word. They tended to me like I was something fractured—soft hands and softer voices, as if I might crumble under their touch. Humans were peculiar that way, drawing conclusions from silence alone.

"How did you leave the palace without notice?" Elisienne asked gently, dabbing a cloth against my back, the scent of bath oils soothing but sharp.

"The window," I said quietly.

"The window?" Her brows shot up. "Why?"

"I thought I saw something... and followed."

"In the nude?"

"Yes," I grumbled, burying my face in my arms as I leaned over the edge of the tub.

"You're lucky you weren't injured—or worse," she scolded, though her tone remained light.

A knock cut through the air, followed by a voice that made my heart stammer in my chest.

"Someone is the talk of the palace, and for once, it is not I." Titus' voice wrapped around me as he entered the bathing chamber. He leaned against the doorframe, gaze sweeping over the scene—Elisienne, me, the water clinging to my skin.

"I suppose it's foolish to expect confession tonight," he teased, a quiet smile touching his lips.

"Lord de Clairvaux insisted twice daily now. Morning and afternoon." she chimed in, ever gentle.

"Twice?" Titus echoed, a mock sigh escaping. "Well, then. You should hurry with your bath, Rylen. The chapel awaits."

"I am ready." I stood, water dripping from my body. Elisienne stepped back respectfully.

"Do you need help dressing, Rylen?" she asked softly.

"No. I can manage, thank you."

Titus kept his gaze averted, addressing her with a nod. "I'll escort him to the chapel, Elisienne. Thank you for your care."

She bowed lightly and exited, leaving only us—Titus and I—between the steam and the silence.

His fingers toyed with the edge of his shirt sleeve before lifting toward me as I dried myself. "Where were you?" he asked, his tone gentle—yet something heavier lingered beneath it.

"A mind-unburdening stroll," I replied plainly, wrapping the linen around my lower as I walked past him. His hand caught my forearm.

"Are you still upset with me for earlier? Did you..." he hesitated, "did you try to leave me?"

My brows drew together. "I would never. I truly needed time to clear my thoughts. Clarity." Carefully chosen truths.

His gaze softened, shoulders easing as I stepped in closer. My hand cupped the side of his face, and he leaned into the touch, his hand rising to rest against mine.

"I do wish to apologize again for accusing you." He lifted my palm to his lips, pressing a kiss into it. "I'm sorry, Rylen."

How could I resist someone who so clearly ached for me the same way I ached for him? How could I ever do harm upon him? Yet Morvena's words still coiled in my mind. This could never truly last. It was fleeting—hidden pleasures, secret joys. And in addition, one of us was promised to die.

"You don't need to apologize," I murmured.

"I do."

"You don't." I laughed quietly, brushing a kiss against the corner of his lips.

"I do," he echoed with a smile, shifting to meet my mouth with his.

"I got you something," he said as he pulled away, crossing to the desk. He lifted a glass jar, corked, filled with golden liquid.

"Remember how I said I'd find something you actually liked the taste of?"

"Yes?" I eyed the jar curiously before taking it.

"I thought maybe you were more drawn to sweet things. And maybe I could make that tea a little more tolerable for you."

"This is what you had in mind?" I turned the jar in my hands, watching as the thick liquid clung to the glass in slow drips—golden and strangely beautiful.

"Here," he said, popping the cork. A thread of the liquid clung to the stopper before snapping off, sticking to his

fingertip. "It's... well, it's sticky," he chuckled, setting the cork aside.

"Well, I'd rather not dirty myself again," I said, taking his wrist. My hand slid up, thumb brushing his palm as I guided his finger to my lips, drawing it in slowly. My tongue pressed against the tip.

The taste bloomed gently on my tongue—warm, golden, like sunlight trapped in nectar. It was rich and smooth, with a subtle floral note that reminded me of blooming lavender kissed by salt air.

I let his finger slip from between my lips.

He cleared his throat, a faint flush coloring his cheeks. "What do you think?"

"I can't tell if it's the thing that's sweet... or if it's you."

To my delight, his blush deepened. His gaze averted for a moment, just as it seemed to always do whenever he was debating with the desire that surged within him. Heat sunk deep within me. A Stiffness from between my legs stirring and pressing against the linen.

"I... I'd suggest you try either the honey or me again, separately," he said, a charming grin tugging at his lips, "but I fear you won't like the taste of me as much."

"If you want me to taste you," I said, dipping my finger into the jar, "you could simply ask."

His breath caught as I traced a line of honey across his lower lip. For a second, I just stared at his glistening lip. I let the anticipation coil tighter, imagination blooming unchecked. Oh, how I wonder how his whole body would look—taste—covered

in this. I leaned in, tongue dragging slowly along the seam before gently tugging his bottom lip between my teeth.

"Rylen..." he whispered, my name a quiet plea.

"I'd say you pair quite nicely," I murmured against his mouth, "so much sweetness—I can't help but crave more." My fingers brushed the fastenings of his shirt. "And with something so messy... one really should be careful." I undid the buttons, baring his chest to the dim, golden light of the room.

I kissed him again, deeper this time, and his hands tangled in my hair. My hand dipped once more into the jar—thick, amber liquid coating my fingers as I let it drip down his chest and over his abdomen, leaving a glistening trail that made him shiver. "I believe I've made a bit of a mess."

His breath hitched as I trailed my fingers lower, tracing below his trousers and over his hardness. "I expect you'll clean it up," he said, voice thick with want.

"Yes, Your Highness," I replied with a languid smile, letting the cloth around me drop as I grabbed his hand and gently guided him onto the bed. The soft thud of his body meeting the mattress sent a spark of something deep and carnal through me. I straddled him, pinning his wrists to the bedding as I hovered above, my tongue dipping into the honey once more.

It truly was the sweetest thing I'd tasted here—but even so, it paled in comparison to him.

I let my tongue wander beyond the trail, circling his nipple, tasting his skin. His hand escaped my hold, fingers cupping my cheek and lifting my face to meet his gaze.

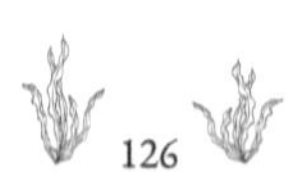

"Rylen," he said with a smile, "you're straying from your task. That honey isn't going to clean itself."

I dipped lower, lips meeting the sticky trail once more, warm and golden against his skin. My tongue swept slowly, deliberately, savoring the mix of sweet and salt as I made my way down his stomach. I traced the edge of where skin met the fabric of his trousers, lips gently teasing. His body responded in quiet tremors, breath catching with every lingering touch.

The air between us thickened with want, his fingers threading into the sheets beneath him. My lips pressed against the thin barrier of his trousers, and I could feel the shape of him, warm and eager beneath the cloth.

I paused, letting my breath fan across him. "May I?" I asked softly, glancing up.

He looked down at me, desire clouding his eyes, his voice barely audible. "You may."

He helped, lifting his hips slightly, and I eased the fabric down. My hand curled around him, tentative but curious. I leaned forward, pressing a soft kiss to his hip, just beside where he pulsed with heat and tension.

My tongue followed the trail I had painted in gold, the honey clinging to his shaft like sunlight caught on flesh. It guided me down the length of him, warm and velvet-soft beneath my lips. He trembled as I tasted the first pearl of him—salt and earth and something sweeter, something that belonged only to him. It was not the honey that lingered—it was Titus. Every note of him, elemental and achingly human.

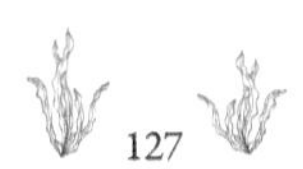

He let out a low moan, hips pressing back into the bedding, the sound slipping from him like prayer. And yet there was nothing sanctified in this—only want, raw and reverent.

I took him into my mouth slowly, feeling the pulse of him against my tongue, the way he seemed to soften and stiffen in the same breath. My fingers traced the lines of his thighs, memorizing the trembling path of his need.

His hand found the back of my head, fingers slipping through the strands of my damp hair. "Look at me," he said—his voice a command softened by plea. "Look at me while you taste my cock, Rylen."

Cock. What a crude word for the appendage—brutal in its syllables, unsoftened by grace. And yet, in that moment, it fit. Crude, human, wanton. I had no other name for it, no other language to wrap around the thing that had undone me with so little effort. *Titus' cock.* The first true indulgence I'd tasted on land. Delectable. Devastating. A vulgar name, yes—but no less sacred for it.

My gaze met his as the tip pressed through the seam of my lips. His eyes locked to mine as I moved, slow and sure, mouth rising and falling in a rhythm we had once learned by hand alone. His grip tightened, knuckles blanching against the bedsheets, the other in my hair. His lips parted, his lashes fluttered, and then—he watched me again. Watched as I worshipped him in a way no prayer could rival.

Need thrummed in my own body, sharp and urgent. I had not allowed myself release since the day it was done by my

own hand. But now, tasting him, watching him unravel—there was nothing left but ache.

My free hand wrapped around myself, fingers curling in time with my mouth's descent. A moan slipped from me, muffled against the heat of him, as the tight coil in my groin began to fray.

Titus' hips moved in time with my mouth, a quiet desperation in the slow rise and fall, until a tremor passed through him—then a breath, shuddered and sharp. He spilled into me, and I drank him in, every drop like some sacred offering. The taste of him lingered.

And then I broke, too—my body tensing as I spilled onto the sheets, silent save for the way my breath caught in my throat. It was not release alone; it was surrender.

"Come to me," he said. His voice was quieter now, steadier, a tether in the quiet.

I rose, limbs heavy and slow with the aftershocks of pleasure. He reached for me, his palm warm against my cheek, and pulled me into a kiss—tasting himself on my lips.

"I love you, Rylen," he whispered, and in his voice I heard not just want but wonder.

For a moment, I could not breathe. I wondered if he knew what such words meant—to speak them out loud in such a way. But when I looked into his eyes, I found no doubt. Only softness. Only truth.

"And I love you, Titus," I said, my voice barely louder than the hush of breath between us. And in that moment, I believed this could be.

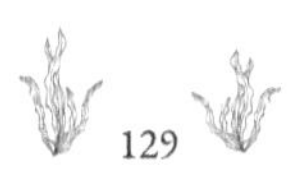

Chapter Seven

"What do you know of merfolk?" I asked, voice quiet against the clink of porcelain, the steam from my morning tea curling and warm.

"Merfolk?" Elisienne's hand stilled mid-stroke, the brush caught in the strands of my hair. Our eyes met in the mirror, hers curious, mine purposely unreadable.

"Yes. Merfolk." I repeated.

She resumed slowly, thoughtful now. "Most folk never see them. Not even the fishermen who live and die by the tides. To them, mer are little more than folklore—fairy tales to entertain children, or cautionary fables to keep them from wandering too close to the sea."

I took another sip. The honey softened the bitterness of the tea, yet somehow the sweetness lingered with an ache I hadn't anticipated. A taste that brought memories unbidden—golden and warm and sticky on the tongue.

"What sort of cautionary tales?"

Her fingers abandoned the brush, combing gently through my hair now. "They say the mer don't come to shore—not willingly. But there are stories. Of sirens, they call them. Twisted creatures with voices spun from longing. Their song, they say, can strip a man of sense and will alike. Make him walk into the sea with a smile on his lips, even as the salt claims his lungs."

"Morvena," I breathed. The seawitch's name escaped before I could stop it.

"Pardon?" she asked, fingers pausing mid-twist.

"Nothing," I murmured, collecting myself. "You said they don't come willingly?"

"Aye," she nodded, continuing to twist my hair with care. "When men see something half-fish, half-human, they see power. Control over storms. Over tides. Over fate, even. Some try to catch them. Tame them. And when they cannot..." Her voice softened, "Well. People can be cruel. That's all I'll say."

My jaw tightened. The cup trembled slightly in my grasp, but I steadied it. "But it's outlawed, is it not? To hunt them here in Gadimore?"

"It is now. Before King Evren sat the throne—when he was still just a prince—he fought for the merfolk. Said they were not beasts, but people. Said they did not harm unless harmed first. That they never invaded the land, so why should we invade the sea? That we should take the little we need and let them be." She smiled faintly. "A noble heart he passed to his son."

"Prince Titus?" I asked, though I already knew the answer.

She nodded. "He sees to the laws. Makes sure our waters remain a sanctuary—for both men and mer. No fisherman is allowed too deep, too far, not where they dwell. And any pirate fool enough to hunt merfolk is punished swiftly. The trade of their tails is outlawed. And keeping them as pets—" she shuddered, "—it's barbaric."

So Titus had not lied.

"When he was little," she added with a small laugh, "he used to say he had merfolk friends. Claimed he spoke to one. A silly thing, but sweet. Children dream such things when they're lonely."

My throat tightened. So we had been friends. Once. But if he had remembered me so well... why had he not kept his promise?

"He is a prince," I said, unable to still the quiet ache that had begun to stir beneath my ribs. "How could he have ever been lonely?"

My question was earnest, but it betrayed something more. Curiosity, yes—but also longing. A need to understand the man behind the crown. My prince.

Elisienne's hands moved more gently now, twisting the strands of my hair with less urgency. "Queen Isolde passed when he was still a boy," she said softly. "She bore no other children who survived the cradle. If Titus was a beam of sunshine, then she was the sky that held him. When she passed, the palace dimmed—and so did he. She had been the only one

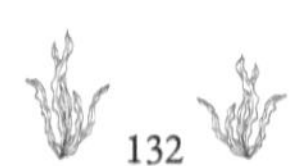

who truly understood him. That's not to say King Evren was lacking—no—but she had a way of grounding him, of listening with genuine interest in all the things he loved. She made space for him in a way no one else did.

For a time, he retreated inward, barely spoke. But little by little, the layers came back—until he resembled himself again. Or rather, a version of himself. Titus was always curious, always thinking too deeply, asking too many questions. The other noble children didn't quite know what to make of him, and I think he learned from that—learned to be less open, learned to wear the image of perfection everyone expected.

He never minded solitude, not at first. But solitude can turn bitter with time. So I believe he shaped a version of himself the world would accept, just so he wouldn't be so alone."

I said nothing. Words had momentarily abandoned me, caught beneath the weight of the image she painted: a boy-prince wrapped in velvet, crowned by birthright, and yet untouched by genuine warmth. Elisienne had watched a boy born of light and wonder dim, then rekindle—only into a reflection of what he had once been.

"But," she continued, a bit too brightly, "he will not be alone much longer. His men are good company, of course, but even his fleet has its limits. Companionship, affection, the duty of heirs—all these things require a woman."

Something in me turned cold. "What do you mean?"

Her pause was brief. "I only say so because it will be announced this afternoon... but while King Evren was in Balthvidae, solidifying peace, part of the treaty included a

union. Prince Titus is to wed their daughter—Princess Seraphina. She arrived at the palace this morning."

The words struck like a blow to the gut.

"W-What?" The sound escaped me too quickly, and far too sharp.

Elisienne gave me a puzzled glance in the mirror. "He is nineteen, long past the age where most nobles are already wed. The King has decided it is time for his son to step away from the sea and begin thinking of the future. Of Gadimore. Of heirs."

Her voice continued, but it faded into a blur, like the tide retreating from shore. All I could feel was the slow, nauseating twist of my insides. Something bitter curled beneath my tongue. My hand trembled as it pressed against my stomach, as though to calm the storm rising inside me. But it did nothing to quiet the dread.

"Where is he?" I asked, though I already feared the answer.

"I believe he's with King Evren and the princess now," she said. "They're discussing the final arrangements, before the announcement—"

I rose before she could finish, the chair scraping sharply against the floor.

"Rylen," Elisienne called after me, startled. "Where are you going?"

But I was already walking, heart pounding in my chest. I had to find him. Had to see him—speak to him. This couldn't be right. He wouldn't—he couldn't—pledge himself to another. Not when only a night ago, he had whispered those words.

134

Not when he had told me *he* loved *me*.

My feet carried me forward without thought, driven by something far deeper than direction—an ache in the center of my chest, not warm like affection, but burning, volatile. A heat that curled tight and trembling beneath my ribs.

My fingers slipped over the talisman strung at my center. Its edges had grown sharper again, the smoothness waning—reverting. Since meeting with Morvena, the change had accelerated. My time here was no longer gently running out; it was collapsing. The tide of my return threatened to pull me under.

And yet, I found myself drawn elsewhere, not to task, not to the king, but to the gardens—those winding, perfumed paths woven like lace through the palace grounds. Something unseen pulled me there. Or perhaps it was not unseen at all, but heard—the low, resonant sound of his laughter, carried on the air like a spell.

I paused at the crest of the stone steps, my gaze catching on the figures below. They had just emerged from a veil of flowering shrubs, the path unfurling behind them like a ribbon toward the central fountain. Every detail—the soft dappling of light on carved stone, the honey-gold petals that lined the walk, the song of distant birds—was too beautiful. Too perfect.

And so was she.

The princess.

Her laughter chimed, soft and elegant, matching the curve of her full lips and the deep rose blooming on her cheeks.

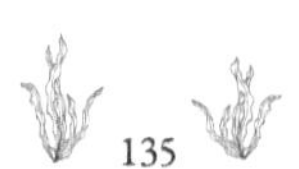

Dark hair curled like ribbons around her shoulders, catching the light in dusky waves. She was exquisite. Regal. Right.

They looked like a painting. One carefully curated by the world to be pleasing. Balanced. Ideal. The kind of portrait a kingdom would cherish and a court would praise. And yet I could not move. Could not tear my gaze away as the man I loved entertained another.

But there was no cruelty in it. No betrayal. He hadn't broken any vow—we had made no promises aloud. And still, it cut.

He kept his hands folded behind his back, respectful, distant, as though unwilling to risk more than polite conversation. His smile was gentle, practiced. Charming even—but not quite real. Not to someone who had studied the sincerity of it in the shadows and quiet confessions. It sat upon his mouth like a borrowed thing. His eyes, too, did not gleam the way they did when he looked at me. When he let himself be himself.

And then his gaze lifted—found me.

Just for a moment. Just long enough.

Surprise flickered there. Then the mask returned with almost painful precision.

"Apologies," he said to the princess. "I forgot I had matters to attend to. I'll see you at the banquet."

His voice was kind, his bow courteous, but his eyes never sought mine again. Not until he passed me, close enough for his fingers to brush against the back of my hand in a featherlight touch. Nothing more. And yet it lit my skin like fire.

"Escort Princess Seraphina to Ambassador Maurice," he instructed a nearby guard, his tone calm, composed. Authority wrapped in warmth.

Only when I heard the palace doors close behind her did I turn. He was already watching me, that calm unraveling now into something more honest—more wounded. The grief in his gaze no longer hidden behind duty or decorum.

"Rylen," he said. My name was a sigh. A surrender.

I swallowed the storm behind my teeth. Kept my voice even. "I wish to attend confession early," I said, my words clipped in their formality, though something trembled beneath them. "Will you accompany me? My mind is too fractured—I have lost my sense of direction."

His expression cracked, only slightly. But enough. "Of course."

We said nothing more. Not as we ascended the stone steps. Not as the heavy doors closed behind us. But our silence was not empty. It was filled with everything we had not said.

The chapel doors groaned shut behind me, the heaviness reverberating through stone and stained glass. The hush that followed was immediate, sacred—a silence that felt like being held underwater, caught somewhere between stillness and suffocation.

I had scarcely crossed the threshold when his hand closed around my wrist, firm and imploring. My body, the traitorous thing that it was, turned into his as if it had been waiting—aching—for the summons. There was no resistance left in me. Not for him.

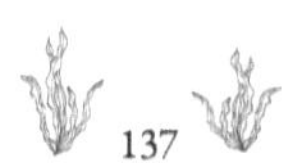

Titus pulled me close, and I let him. His warmth encircled me like sunlight breaking through a winter sky—too bright, too brief. I breathed him in. The scent of him, of the sandalwood and the sea that clung to his skin like memory. It nearly soothed the raw ache blooming inside my chest. Nearly.

His palm rose to my cheek, guiding my gaze to his. His other arm curved behind me, keeping me within the compass of him. So near that I could feel the shape of his breath against my mouth, but not close enough to taste it. Our lips, a hairsbreadth apart. The space between us taut.

He looked at me—not with hunger, not with apology, but with that same quiet awe he had always reserved for me. As if I were something holy. Something worthy.

I hated it.

"Why do you always look at me as though I am something precious?" I asked, the question tearing its way from my throat, too soft, too brittle.

"Because you are."

His lips met mine, soft as a secret—but I did not return the gesture. Could not.

"You are promised to another," I whispered, cool and composed, even as the words blistered my tongue. I reached up and removed his hand from my cheek, though the act felt like the peeling away of skin.

He recoiled only slightly, reluctant to release me entirely. His fingers ghosted along my side as if afraid I might vanish should he let go.

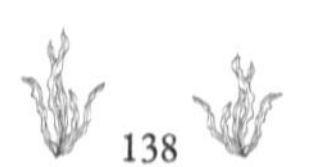

"I am a prince," he said, voice measured. "I have always been promised."

"Then why—" my voice broke before I gathered it again, sharp as splintered coral, "—why did you tell me you loved me?"

"I... I thought you knew what this was." His voice stumbled. "Rylen, if I have misled you—if I allowed you to believe this could be more than what it is—I am sorry. I meant it when I said I love you. My heart—gods, it is yours. But I thought we understood. I have obligations. A duty I cannot forsake." He hesitated then, eyes flicking toward mine, uncertain. "I shouldn't have assumed, I suppose... given that you—"

"That I?" The words came out clipped, brittle with the effort it took not to spit them. "Do you believe me ill as well, then? Touched by madness for daring to hope?"

He flinched, not from the sharpness in my voice but, I think, from the wound he'd cut into me without meaning to. "No. Of course not," he said, softer now, as if gentleness could bind what had already begun to break. "Rylen, I am not so blind as they think me. I do not know what you are. Not entirely. But I have always known you are not of this place. And yet I never asked. I never needed to. Because by the time I saw the strangeness in you, I had already fallen."

My heart gave a throb, as if it might tear itself from my ribs and offer itself to him, still beating. And still, I could not make sense of the pain.

"I do not understand." My voice was quieter now, but not steadier. "I understand I was never promised your hand.

That this world would never grant me your name or your throne. But if you always knew you belonged to someone else—why would you ever give me your heart?"

The silence that followed was unkind.

Perhaps our mistake was believing love to be enough.

Among my kind, love was not a matter of politics or obligation. It was rare, fierce, and final. We did not fall idly. We did not love by halves. And when we did, it was for life.

Though Titus and I had not completed the rites, some part of me had already begun to bind itself to him, quiet as barnacles growing around the bones of a shipwreck. I had imagined the moment—how it might feel to become one beneath moonlit waves, to press my forehead to his and feel the sacred weaving of souls.

But that was the truth of my world, not his.

In this kingdom, love bowed before lineage. Devotion came second to diplomacy. I was not a prince here, only a curiosity. A passerby swept up in someone else's story. A creature that did not quite belong on land or in court.

And worse still—I was a man.

That alone made our love a kind of defiance. A quiet rebellion whispered behind closed doors, with hands held in shadow. Had they known what I truly was—what blood sang beneath my skin—they would not have whispered.

They would have hunted.

Humans did not see my kind as beloveds. They saw us as marvels. As trophies. As bodies to bind and gawk at. Merfolk were not consorts. We were collections.

And still... I had dared to dream with him.

What a fool I was, to believe that love alone could unmake a world built on chains.

"Tell me, Prince," I said, my palms splaying against the firm line of his chest, the warmth of him beneath my skin a final indulgence before I forced myself back. One step. Then another. "What am I to you?"

My voice, though even, trembled at its root.

"A dalliance to sate curiosity? A rebellion you wear in secret, thrilling only so long as no one sees it? Will you cast me aside once you've lain with your princess—when duty calls and the thrill of disobedience fades?"

My breath shivered in my throat.

"Why are you here, Titus?" I asked, quieter now, but no less cutting. "Why linger in this chapel with me, when she waits with a crown and heirs in her future? Go to her. End this, and let me return to where I belong."

Tell me it meant nothing. Tell me this was only a moment of warmth. A curiosity. A mistake. Lie to me. Tell me I was never real—so I might tear myself from you completely. So I might forget I ever felt like more. Make resent you. Make me hate you.

He stood still, statuesque in the quiet, as though his very breath might shatter us.

"If I could be with you," he began, and oh, how gently his voice broke over the words, "I would. In a heartbeat, Rylen, I would be yours."

A pause. A pivot. The air shifted like a storm pulling in from the sea.

"But I cannot," he said, gaze flicking away—not to me, but to the carved figure of Valtherion standing vigil at the center. "I have obligations. Expectations. What we have..."

He cleared his throat, "It is unsightly. Unnatural."

And though the words were spoken by his tongue, they did not wear his voice. They were too flat. Too practiced. They belonged to councilmen and cloistered priests, to kings who bartered sons like coin.

He did not look at me when he said it. And that, more than anything, made me tremble.

"So," he continued, his tone gone cold, royal, rote. "You are right. Let us be done with this, Rylen."

I swallowed against the rising tide in my throat. This was what I had asked for—what I needed. And yet... Yet my heart still reached for him like a drowning man for a passing ship.

"Y-You find what we share to be... unsightly?" My voice cracked. The words slipped out raw, unguarded, and with them came the sting behind my eyes—a pressure I could no longer contain, welling up like seawater against a broken gate.

"No," he said, and his voice was all but breath, too fragile for the false cruelty he had tried to conjure moments before. His eyes found mine—wet now, shining, the fleeting coldness having collapsed beneath the weight of truth.

"Does this feel unnatural to you?" I asked, stepping into the space between us once more.

He shook his head, wordless at first, as if the very question wounded him.

"No," he whispered again, with more conviction this time.

"Then what," I breathed, "could possibly be unvirtuous about our love?"

His chest rose, trembled. Silence passed like a shadow between us.

"Nothing," he answered at last. His lower lip gave the faintest tremble, betraying all the agony his station demanded he suppress. "Nothing."

He reached for me, not to hold, but to touch, reverently, like one might graze a relic.

"Absolutely nothing," he said again, voice soaked in sorrow. "Our love is sacrosanct. It pales all else, Rylen."

"*Sacrosanct?*" I echoed, the word ghosting from my lips, barely a breath. My hand rose of its own accord, fingers trembling as they found his cheek. I wiped the tear that lingered there.

"Yes," he murmured, leaning into the touch. "Sacrosanct." His arms slipped around me, drawing me close until the rest of the world blurred into irrelevance. "I am sorry," he whispered, voice muffled against my skin. "To be virtuous is to be true to one's nature. And this—us—this is what I know to be true."

His breath stirred against my mouth, asking rather than assuming. "May I?"

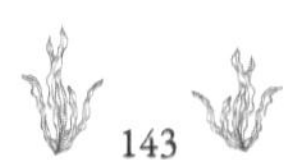

"You may," I answered, and in the same breath I met him, lips to lips.

There was nothing timid in him then. His fingers tangled into my hair as his mouth claimed mine. His kiss was hungry, edged with a desperation I knew all too well—the desperation of hearts pressed against inevitability. His body bore down on mine, forcing a step back until the soft thud of wood against my thighs marked our descent into fever.

His hands found my hips, possessive and trembling, pulling me flush against him. I felt him then—his cock straining against mine, both imprisoned by fabric that suddenly felt cruel in its purpose.

"Run away with me," he gasped, lips brushing mine as he spoke.

"What?"

"Let us flee to where love is not something to hide or bind. I do not want this to be ephemeral. I want forever. The crown is ash in my hands without you."

My breath faltered. "And of your fleet?"

"They will find another. My command is not what defines me. If the sea calls to me, I would rather sail it with you beside me. All of it, Rylen. The world, the quiet days, the storms—I want them all, but only if you are there. We could leave tonight. I'll endure the banquet, wear the mask one last time, and then—no more lies, no more duty. Only us."

I kissed him again—soft, silencing.

I wanted to tell him yes. That I would. That I could. But I could not. The cords of my fate were already knotted by

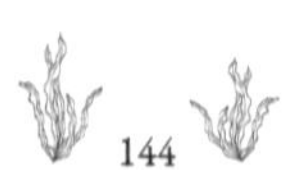

another. Even if I severed my deal with Morvena, the truth lingered: he was of land, I of sea. We were never meant to last beyond the dream of what could be.

And yet—I said the words anyway.

"I'll run away with you," I whispered, choosing—for a single, stolen moment—to believe.

His smile against my mouth was like the sun breaking through storm clouds. But it faltered into a gasp as my hand slid beneath the fabric of his breeches and wrapped around his cock, slow and deliberate.

"Rylen—" His voice was low, frayed at the edges. "We oughtn't... not here. Valtherion—" His gaze flicked over my shoulder to the stone-carved god, noble and unmoving in his sanctified stillness.

"Titus..." My voice was velvet and heat. "My body yearns for you. Will you deny me now?"

"Y-Yearns?" His cheeks flushed crimson.

I said nothing, only turned away and lowered my trousers, baring myself in the quiet hush of the chapel. I heard his breath catch. Then his warmth enveloped me—arms encircling my waist, lips brushing against the nape of my neck.

"Are you sure?" he asked, already undoing the ties of my tunic slowly.

I closed my eyes, resting my head back against his shoulder.

"I have never longed for anything as I do for you. I want you, Titus. All of you."

I wanted to give myself to the one I should never have touched—and would never stop loving. The longing had grown unbearable, blooming from the center of me like a tide swelling against the shore. I wanted to make a bond of it, a vow unspoken but etched into flesh. I wanted to be his. Not in name, not in title—but in spirit, in breath, in the sacred places that love hides.

"Rylen," Titus murmured, pressing against me, his heat stark and shivering down my spine. "I do not want to hurt you."

His voice trembled at the cusp of restraint. Then, with a low breath and a murmur of apology, his warmth left me. My hands gripped the edge of the pew before me. Perhaps it was a sign. Perhaps we should stop. But before the thought could gather shape, he returned.

"It's meant for anointing during rites," he murmured from behind me, voice low, almost sheepish. "But I doubt the priest will notice if it's used... for something else entirely."

I turned just slightly, eyes catching the glint of glass in his hand—a ceremonial decanter trembling slightly as he uncorked it. The faint earthy aroma of something rich and pressed filled the air. Oil, thick and golden, pooled into his palm as he poured it slowly. And then his hand moved down, spreading it over himself, his breath catching as the oil coated his cock. A moan through clenched teeth. A quiet curse.

Then I felt it—cool at first, then warm as it was worked between my cleft, his fingers slick and unhurried as he eased the way. The intimacy of it—the care—nearly undid me.

He leaned in, the solid weight of him at my back, one hand braced beside mine, the other steadying himself.

"If you want me to stop," he whispered, lips brushing the curve of my ear, "say so."

I could not speak, so I nodded.

There was a press—tentative, searching—and my breath caught in my throat. He pushed forward gently, my body's resistance taut. It ached—sharp, intimate, unfamiliar—but I bore it, my fingers curling around the pew as I exhaled through it.

"You're so tight," he breathed, voice wrecked with wonder and restraint. "Does it hurt?"

"No," I managed, voice thin. "Keep going, Titus."

And so he did. Patient at first, easing deeper with each pulse of breath. Pain ebbed, dulled by the slow rise of pleasure that crept beneath my skin like the first rays of sun through water. When he began to move—truly move—it was with something instinctive. My hips moved back in time with his, a rhythm that soon lost all ceremony and became something intrinsic. Wordless. Needful.

I looked back over my shoulder, catching him in half-shadow. His lips parted, lashes heavy, jaw clenched. And oh, he was beautiful like this—unguarded, undone.

His hand found my chin, lifting it, and then his lips met mine—an open, desperate kiss that spoke of more than just desire. It was longing. It was love made flesh. The tempo of his body quickened, and I met it, lost in the way we found each other again and again in motion and moan.

His other hand wrapped around me, stroking in time with his thrusts. And when I fell, *I fell utterly*—spilling into his hand with a cry I could not silence. A heartbeat later, I felt him still, then tremble, then press deep and shudder with release. I was filled, completely and fully.

We remained there, a tangle of sweat and breath and silence. His forehead rested between my shoulders, our chests rising together as though we shared lungs. And then his arms gathered me close, pulling me into his hold, his heart drumming against my back.

"Nothing in my mind could have compared to this," he said softly.

"Did you think of this often?" I asked, smiling faintly.

"Yes," he laughed—quiet, sheepish. "I've thought of taking you. Of you taking me. More times than I should admit."

I nestled closer, letting his warmth fold around me. In that moment, the world could end, and I would not mourn it. For I had known what it meant to be loved—wholly, fiercely, and without shame.

Chapter Eight

The scent of lavender and orange blossom clung to the air as I stepped into the banquet hall. The echo of my footsteps lost beneath the quiet scurry of servants moving to and fro, silver platters in hand, wine carafes poised for pouring. They danced around one another in a silent choreography, adding the final flourishes before the court arrived.

Light spilled in from the towering windows high above, the room glowing with a softness from it. Shimmering constructs of iron and crystal suspended like tangled stars, gleamed like dew on spider silk, casting trembling reflections onto polished marble floors.

The tables were long, dark wood draped in embroidered cloth and garlands of soft blooms—pale roses, foxglove, and trailing vines. It was beautiful. Almost cruelly so.

I stepped further in, uncertain of my place among so much purpose, and was met by the faint tap of heels that preceded Elisienne's voice.

"Ah, there you are." She appeared beside me as if conjured from the shadows. "You've arrived early. Good. That gives us a moment before the rest of the court descends."

She glanced toward the tables, her sharp eyes assessing the arrangement with a practiced eye. "You will be seated with the Prince's fleet." Elisienne stepped lightly toward one of the long tables, gesturing faintly. "Along with the officers and their chosen guests."

"And Titus?"

She gave a small smile, not unkind. "He'll be seated beside the princess. Of course. At the high table—just there." She nodded toward the elevated platform where a shorter, richly adorned table overlooked the rest. "The king will sit central. On his right, the Balthvidae ambassador. On his left, the princess. Titus beside her."

I nodded.

The light from the windows had begun to deepen, a dark mix of purple and red now. A bell sounded somewhere in the distance, faint and slow—calling the court to gather.

I took my seat among men who believed I was one of their own—shoulder to shoulder with sailors and captains, their laughter low and briny. They trickled in slowly, like the swell of a rising tide, creeping into a hidden cove. Yet I scarcely registered them. My gaze wandered—no, hunted. Searching for

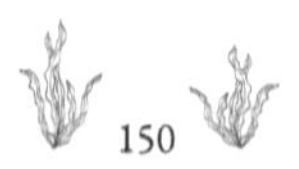

what had never truly belonged to me, and yet still, somehow, felt like mine.

I felt him before I saw him. A ripple through the air, a tug beneath my sternum, like a current calling me home. My heart startled in my chest, then shifted to a different rhythm entirely, one it had learned from him.

Then our eyes met.

He was devastating.

Even now, beneath the weight of duty, dressed in royal finery, he still managed to take my breath. I had to still my hands against the edge of the table, steady my breathing so I wouldn't gawk like some lovesick boy dragged in from the wilds.

Titus walked with grace that came not from breeding, but from battle. Every inch of him carved in purpose, but his smile when he offered it to the princess at his side, was a betrayal of softness. He escorted her gently, attentively. And yet not once did I miss the quick flick of his gaze, the dart of green that found mine again.

Then the king entered. Evren Beaumir. The man I had come to kill. He was broader than I had imagined, regal not just in stature, but in something unspoken—an invisible tether that seemed to draw every eye, and bend the very air around him. I saw Titus in him. The tilt of the jaw, the striking emerald eyes, the nobility of posture that made others straighten in their seats. He wore his crown like it was part of his anatomy. It startled me, how handsome he was, how... kind his eyes looked.

This was the monster?

This was the supposed tyrant my people had bled beneath. The reason I had climbed from the deep, carrying secrets and storms in my chest.

But none of that mattered now.

Not if I couldn't bring myself to kill his son.

King Evren stepped forward, his hands splayed upon the royal table, voice stilling the room without needing to rise. "I want to thank you all for joining us for this special occasion."

A pause. A smile that did not dim the conviction in his tone.

"As we know, Gadimore and Balthvidae have long been divided—by sea, by land, by history. But tonight we celebrate the beginning of a union long in the making. Prince Titus of Gadimore and Princess Seraphina of Balthvidae. Two kingdoms, two bloodlines, bound together for the prosperity of our continent."

Lopharius. Stronger. United.

The words continued, ceremonial and proud, but I heard only the rushing in my ears.

Titus watched his father with rapt attention, the portrait of a perfect heir. Composed. Loyal. Obedient. And then, just as the king lifted his cup to seal the toast, Titus' gaze found mine again.

It burned.

A quiet, blistering thing that made my breath catch. My cheeks flushed with the shame of wanting, of needing something I had no claim to. I dropped my eyes. I couldn't look at him.

He was not truly mine.

No matter what our time together had meant. No matter how his mouth had shaped my name in reverence, or how my body still ached where he had touched me as if he had written himself into my very bones.

I was his, but he wasn't mine.

And I hated the truth of it—that he had settled somewhere behind my ribs, that I could not unmake the tether between us. I had come here to take a life. To avenge. But the moment I had recognized his soul, I knew I would not raise a hand against him, nor his father. Not even for justice.

I would not become the monster in his story.

If it cost me my life, so be it. Better that than his love.

And so I turned my face from him, shoulders held straight. I told myself I was only here for the pageantry, for the final gesture before I slipped away. He had a kingdom. He had a future. And I had a bargain to fulfill. A prince's heart had been promised. It was time to pay the due.

I had just begun to rise, fingers brushing the hem of my tunic, when the great banquet doors groaned open with such suddenness that the very air inside the hall seemed to seize. The rustle of silk and whispered conversation stilled, as if the room itself had paused its breath.

A guard stepped in first, his posture taut with urgency, each stride cutting through the perfumed haze like a blade. All eyes followed him as he approached the royal table, and then behind him another figure emerged. Older. Frayed at the edges but not undone. His beard unkempt, his uniform stained with

salt and ash, yet he carried himself with the stubborn dignity of a man who had defied death and returned with the remnants of the sea still clinging to his skin.

"That's Captain Roland LeVesque," someone murmured, the name slipping through the air like a prayer, or a curse.

"He's alive."

The words struck like thunder behind my ribs. I turned my gaze to Titus. The guard leaned in to whisper something into his ear, and I watched the subtle shift of his face—thoughtful, alert. And then his eyes found mine. Steady. Searching.

Had I been discovered?

My breath thinned, the walls pressing close around me. I looked to the Captain again, scouring his face—lined and weary, but unfamiliar. Perhaps time had altered him, or perhaps the guilt had blurred my memory of his. So many faces had looked up at me beneath the waves. So many I had let the ocean claim.

I could not stay. My chair scraped gently against the stone as I slipped away, quiet and quick. No one stopped me. Why would they? I was a ghost at this table, a fiction seated among the living.

But as I crossed the threshold, I made the mistake of glancing back—and there he was. Titus, rising from his seat, his gaze locked to mine. There was something in it—concern, confusion, perhaps even grief. And for a heartbeat, I faltered.

But then I ran.

I slipped through the palace corridors like a shadow chasing its last light, my path winding toward the stables. The air was cooler there, laced with the breath of beasts and the musk of hay. I moved among the horses with unsteady steps, unsure, unknowing. But she was there... Brisa. Familiar. Tolerant. She turned her head toward me.

I reached for her gently, murmuring nonsense to soothe my own heart more than hers. She didn't flinch as I touched her neck, didn't pull away as I fumbled with the reins hanging on the wooden post, copying the motions I'd seen Titus perform. My fingers trembled but held.

The weight of her hooves echoed as I led her out into the fading day, each clack on the cobblestones a beat closer to freedom. Mounting her was another matter. My limbs were not made for this. My muscles protested. But somehow, I pulled myself up, clutching to her mane and the reins.

"Go," I whispered. "Please. Go."

And she did.

With a lurch, we sprang forward, the force jolting through me like lightning in my spine. My knees clamped around her too tightly, my balance poor. Brisa tossed her head as though annoyed with me already. But still, she ran. And I learned. Each stride taught me something new about how not to fall.

We passed through the great portcullis, the gates still open. The guards didn't stop me. Perhaps they didn't know to.

I followed the sun. *West,* I told myself. West to the Aserian Sea. To home. To Morvena. To the end of this war inside me.

The sun bled across the sky like a wound torn open, its golden light catching on the curves of the talisman pressed to my chest. The once-smooth glass was nearly coarse now. Time, like the tide, was turning against me. If I died before reaching the sea, the sea would still claim him. That was the nature of our magic. It did not care for intention, only for the keeping of promises.

"Rylen!"

The voice came as a whisper first, riding on the wind. Then louder.

"Rylen!"

I turned. Titus' figure approached fast—his horse built for pursuit, and he for command. He was gaining, swift as a wave rushing toward shore. I urged Brisa onward, my legs digging in, my voice frantic. "Faster!"

She obeyed—too well. We jolted forward, her pace breaking rhythm, careening now. We veered from the path, branches clawing at us as the forest encroached. The terrain grew jagged. Roots snaked through the underbrush like bones beneath flesh. I clung to her back, barely seated, slipping with every bounce.

A cry tore from my throat as she stumbled—her hoof catching on a stone, or a rut I hadn't seen. Her weight shifted. I was flying and then falling.

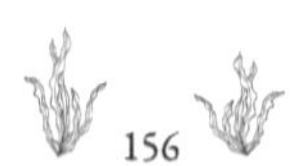

The world spun and the thud that followed came sharp, final. My back met the ground, and the breath was knocked from me like the sea had crashed into my lungs. I stared up at the darkening sky, the branches above weaving into a web that trembled with the wind.

Somewhere, I heard Brisa whinny.

Somewhere, I heard his voice again.

"Rylen!"

But I couldn't answer. All I could think of was how far the sea still was and how my prince shouldn't be here. How I should have never been here.

Titus emerged through the blur of branches and dusk, his silhouette haloed by the dying light. He didn't speak at first, just looked at me. The ache in his gaze cleaved deeper than any blade. And then, quietly, as if the words were heavier than he could bear:

"You left me."

There was no tremble in his voice, no desperation—only a measured sorrow, tight and controlled, like a dam on the verge of rupture. The tenderness I'd once seen in his eyes was gone, replaced by something hollowed and raw, a grief that wore the face of anger.

He crouched beside me. His fingers, calloused and warm, found my jaw. Not rough, but not gentle either—his grip was the kind that demanded truth. He tilted my face toward his, forcing my gaze to hold his own.

"You left me," he said again, and this time, the restraint cracked. "Do you not love me anymore? Was it because of what

we did?" His throat bobbed as he swallowed, his eyes gleaming with the threat of tears. "Did I hurt you?"

Pain pulled at my every joint as I forced myself to sit, but I reached for him, my fingers curling in the fabric over his heart. I dragged him into me, wincing as his weight met mine and his knees hit the earth. I held him close, as if I could quiet the storm in him simply by tethering him to my chest.

"Stop," I whispered. "Please. Don't look at me like that."

I only ever wanted you to be happy, I thought, but I couldn't give it voice. Some truths weren't meant to be spoken aloud—they withered when touched by air.

His arms wound around me with urgency, his face burying into the curve of my neck like a man returning to shore after a shipwreck.

"Why did you leave without me?" he asked, his voice muffled, frayed. "Why didn't you wait for me?"

I let my hand trail up, brushing his hair back, needing to see his eyes again. "I promise," I said, "I'll tell you everything. All of it. But only if you take me to the sea. My time is running out, Titus."

I didn't know if he saw the truth in my face or felt it through the pulse in my fingers, but he didn't argue.

"Okay," he said simply, as he exhaled and began to gather the pieces of himself. He stood with a quiet grace and offered his hand to me. "Brisa's too weary to go on. She's not meant for riding like that. We'll take mine."

His tone held no cruelty, but it lacked the warmth I had come to rely on like breath. And his gaze... it skirted mine entirely.

I had done this. I'd known it would wound him, but I had not been prepared to watch him bleed.

I took his hand. He pulled me up carefully. I caught myself against him once more as we rode. My arms wrapped tight around his torso as I pressed my cheek against his back, inhaling the scent of him—cotton, sandalwood and something sweet. My fingers curled into his shirt as I listened to the steady beat of his heart beneath.

This would be the last time I would hold him like this. Even now, with my world falling to pieces around me, I wanted to memorize the rhythm of him. Even when I didn't deserve him.

And so, I clung to him.

For just a moment longer.

The moon lay low in the sky, swollen and silver, casting its glow across the sea like a hand outstretched in welcome. The tide whispered to me in a tongue older than the stars, each wave curling closer to shore as if to brush against my skin and beckon me home. My boots sank into the softened sand, each step heavier than the last, until I stood at the water's edge.

"I have brought you to the sea," Titus said at last, his voice shattering the hush the ocean had draped around us. "Now will you tell me why you left me?"

I did not answer him. Not yet. Instead, I bent in silence, loosening the leather from my feet. The tide licked at me again, more eager this time, like a lover reuniting after too long parted. I walked a step further into its embrace.

Titus followed, careful in his distance, as though unsure if I would disappear entirely should he step too close.

"Our story was never meant to go further than this," I said, watching the moonlight tremble on the surface of the sea. "This place where tide meets land, where my world ends and yours begins."

"I do not understand," he murmured, his brow knitting with a gentleness that nearly undid me.

"You were right to suspect I wasn't of this world." I glanced toward him, finding his eyes already on me. "What gave me away?"

"I told you once—everything sings," he said, voice low and careful. "And when we met, there was a melody in you I couldn't place. Familiar. Haunting. I thought perhaps you were an arcanist, charming me with glamour. So I let you near, curious... But as time passed, I realized it wasn't an enchantment. I thought then perhaps fae. But then I felt the way water bent around you in the spring. Siren was where my mind went."

He stepped forward, and the tide licking at his boots. His hand reached for mine, fingers brushing the back of it

before gently twining with mine. "But I thought you couldn't be a siren," he whispered. "They're said to lure, to destroy. To kill. And you... you've never harmed me."

"But I have," I said, the words thick on my tongue. I waited for his hand to fall away—but it didn't. I swallowed hard. "Before I knew it was you—before I understood what this was—I gave your life away, Titus. I bargained your heart to another. I made promises in ignorance and anger."

His hand tensed in mine. "You promised my life?" His voice was soft. Distant. Bruised.

"*Rylen.*"

Morvena's voice slithered into my mind, cold and sweet. "*You've brought me my heart, then. Well done, little prince.*"

I did not answer her. Instead, I let go of Titus and pushed him back from the sea. From me. "Stay back," I said, lifting my hands. "I beg you, do not touch the sea tonight. If there's even a fragment of love left in you for me—*please*. Don't follow."

He stared at me, wounded. The hurt in his gaze struck harder than any blade.

"Rylen..."

"I made a promise to deliver your heart and I must keep it." My fingers ghosted across my chest, as if they might still the aching beneath. "But what I did not understand—what I could not understand—was why my own heart refused to obey me. Why it quickened when you drew near. Why it sang a different song, one only you seemed to awaken."

My gaze found his, trembling with the weight of truth. "I know now. This traitorous heart of mine... it is not mine at all." A breath caught in my throat. "It beats for you, Titus. It has always been yours."

I hadn't known what we'd done, not truly. But in those stolen moments when breath tangled with breath and silence stretched soft between our sighs, I had already bound myself to him. Unseen threads pulled taut, soul laced to soul. We had bonded. Irrevocably. In a way only my kind ever could.

And yet, he was the one fate had placed just beyond reach, as if to mock me with the shape of what I could not keep. Merfolk bond but once. A single heartbeat claimed. A single soul entwined.

To lose him now would be to live as half a thing—adrift, hollow, condemned to roam the sea with yearning carved into my bones. No, I would not bear that. I would rather die a thousand deaths than return to the sea and ache for the other half of myself. And besides... his soul—his sweet, virtuous soul—deserved to live. Even if not beside me. Even if I was the storm he had to forget in order to find the sun again.

My fingers found the talisman at my throat. I yanked—hard—and it broke free with a sound like bones snapping. The magic recoiled, snapping taut as I flung it to the sand.

He moved toward me then, his lips already parting to speak, to beg. But I didn't let him. Before his words could reach me, I turned and summoned the sea. It answered like a lover

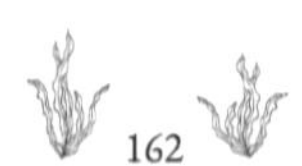

starved. The water rose, seized me by the waist, and pulled me under.

Salt stung my throat. My tears joined the ocean.

And then it began. The sea had claimed me once more. The transformation was never kind. My skin burned with returning scales, my lungs collapsed and gave way to gills. Every inch of me was undone and remade, a prince unmade and reborn in a cradle of sorrow. Fabric tore from my limbs in streaming ribbons, trailing behind me as my body bent to the will of the tide. Bone cracked beneath skin, reshaping with excruciating grace, until the familiar weight of my tail coiled beneath me once more.

Then came the cold—an ancient, knowing cold, not the kind that bites, but one that claims. It slithered in ribbons of shadowed current, slick and serpent-like, coiling about my limbs. And then the yank—sudden, merciless.

Another.

And another.

I was being dragged downward, deeper into the dark where even moonlight feared to follow. To the abyss. My tail thrashed, lashing like a snared thing. But resistance only gave the current more to seize, to wound, to consume.

My hands clawed at the water, desperate, futile.

Then—there. A shift. A tremor of warmth in the sea's eternal hush.

A song.

His song.

I felt him before I saw him—his presence cutting through the cold like the echo of sun on glass. And then he was there, breaching the surface above, arms outstretched, the lines of his body forged in moonlight and will. He was swimming to me, down into the dark. Down where he did not belong.

No. My scream curled inward like a dying star, voiceless and burning. *I told you not to follow. I begged you to stay ashore, to let me go.*

You fool. You beautiful, stubborn fool.

His fingers were almost within reach. So close I could see the tremble in his lashes, the strain in his mouth as he fought against a world not made for him.

Then the final pull. The sea seized me like a jealous lover, cruel and unrelenting, wrenching me downward with a force that fractured thought. Titus vanished above me, swallowed by blue and memory. And I fell into Morvena's domain, into the endless dark that waits at the bottom of my promise.

Chapter Nine

Titus

I had never feared the sea.

Many men tremble at the unknown, shrinking from what they cannot grasp, cannot name. But I—perhaps foolishly, perhaps blessedly—believed that one need not understand something to love it. As a boy, I had learned that if you simply listened, if you stood still and let the world speak, it would tell you everything you needed to know. Beauty, I discovered, often lived in the hush between chaos and calm.

It was that quiet, that knowing, that had always drawn me to the water. And now, it was what drew me into it—chest first, heart open—as Rylen disappeared beneath the waves.

Our story began where the tide meets, but I refused to let it end there. Not now, not when I had finally found the source of the melody that had haunted my soul since I was a child. That day on the shore, I had wandered off again, chasing whispers my ears could hear but no one else cared to tune into. I

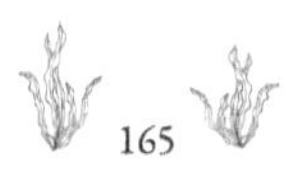

knew Elisienne would scold me, my parents would fret and fuss, but I could not resist the pull. That song, gods, that sweet and aching song. It had lured me past the dunes and down the jagged rocks, where the tide kissed the moss.

And there he was.

Not just a child's imagination. Not a trick. But a boy, beautiful and strange, with eyes the color of a deep-sea hush, a blue so fathomless it threatened to drown thought itself. Scales shimmered faintly across his cheeks and shoulders, like silverleaf scattered by the wind, catching the sunlight in glimmers. And trailing behind him, half-hidden in the tidepool's cradle, was a tail—sleek, powerful, and iridescent, awash in every shade of blue the ocean had ever dreamed.

He did not flee when I approached. He did not startle. He simply looked at me, as if I were not strange or trespassing. We said nothing at first. We watched turtle hatchlings make their perilous journey across the sand, tiny, trembling things seeking home. And then, without effort, we spoke. We laughed. We played. Just two boys.

And now, years later, I followed that same melody, on the same shore once more.

The sea was a cathedral of cold and shadow. It swallowed sound, swallowed breath. But I pressed on, arms cutting through the current, lungs burning. Somewhere ahead, bathed in fractured moonlight, was Rylen—*my Rylen*—his body pulled by something I could not see clearly. I pushed harder. Deeper. And then I heard it.

A new song.

No, not new—wrong. *Twisted.* A discordant thread in an otherwise divine symphony. The sea sang in layers, in colours and shapes and memories, but this—this one strand was venom. It coiled around Rylen like a promise made with a poisoned tongue, pulling him farther from me, dragging him into the depths.

My lungs burned. My eyes stung with salt and pressure, the sea pressing in from all sides, relentless and cold. Humans were not meant to wander so deep—not unless they wished to surrender to the hush of a watery grave.

But my arcane stirred within me, like a coiled thread of warmth against the cold. It listened, it reached—tuning itself to the rhythm of the deep, and by sheer will alone, I breathed. My vision cleared, sharpened by the stillness I summoned. The sea was not my home, no, but she could be kind to those who approached with reverence. If you listened, if you stilled your pulse and quieted your fear, she would show you the way.

Lanternfish appeared drifting toward me on silver fins, their soft glow illuminating the dark like stars adrift in ink. They guided me downward, their light pulsing with my own heartbeat.

Then came a current, sharp and sudden, a wall of resistance that struck my chest like a warning. It pushed against me, insistent. Do not follow. Do not descend.

But I did. I pressed onward, drawing upon the stillness within me to soothe the waters, to ease the fury of the tide. My arcane coiled outward, calming what I could, even as the darkness below grew heavier. The lanternfishes dimmed, their

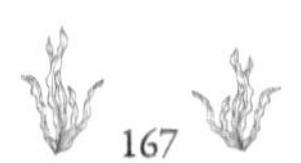

light faltering—as though even their bravery had reached its end.

The silence deepened. Sound was sparse down here—no whalesong, no chatter of distant reefs—only two melodies remained: the twisted, writhing song of something ancient and cruel, and the aching note that had always been Rylen.

A grasp firm against my waist, forced my body to turn as it entrapped me. "Titus," he said, brows drawn tight with worry. "I told you to remain."

"Rylen," I breathed, and to my wonder, the sound carried in the water between us, tender and fragile.

Then came another voice. "The Prince of Gadimore," it echoed, bodiless, curling around us like mist. The last glow of the lanternfishes extinguished, leaving us shrouded in dark. Only a distant flicker of green—soft, eerie—clung to a coral structure ahead.

I pulled Rylen to me, my arms tightening as if I could hold him against what approached.

"You look so much like your father," the voice purred. Feminine, lilting, and steeped in venomous fondness. My gaze searched the shadows, but there was nothing there. Only the weight of her presence, pressing down on me. "How is Evren?" she asked, as if inquiring after an old friend.

"Let Titus leave," Rylen said, his voice sharp, desperate, his palm resting against my chest. He stared into the abyss, eyes fixed on a darkness I could not see. "I won't give you what you asked for. So take me instead. That was the bargain."

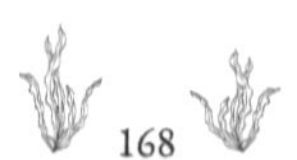

"Shh, my dear cousin," she cooed. "I'm trying to speak."

His lips moved again, but no sound came.

A chill crawled down my spine. "H-How do you know my father?" I asked, my voice barely more than a whisper—but still it carried.

"Let me tell you a tale," she said. "There once was a little mermaid. Her mind was brimming with curiosity, but her heart—oh, her heart was a hollow thing, aching for more. Though she dwelled among treasure and adoration, though coral palaces crowned her days and songbirds of the sea serenaded her nights, the emptiness within her would not be silenced.

So she did the unthinkable. She swam upward—up and up and up—until she breached the surface of her world and gazed upon another. A ship."

I felt a chill crawl across my spine like the touch of a ghost.

"She saw them... humans. And how curious, that they should carve into their vessels the likeness of the very beings they feared. This one bore a figurehead—stunning in craft—a mermaid, crowned in shells, arms outstretched, reaching for the stars above her."

Merella's Vow.

The words echoed like a hymn in my mind. My father's ship. I knew the figurehead well—it depicted Merella herself, the ancient myth, a fairytale told among sailors and children. When the sea was young and lonely, she had gazed too long at the stars. And one star, Merella, seeing the sorrow of the sea, fell

in love. She plummeted from the heavens and surrendered her fire, transforming into the first mermaid. She vowed to remain with the sea forever, and from that vow, the merfolk were born.

The voice continued, peeling away memory and myth.

"Though they warned her the humans were dangerous, she could not look away. There was one among them—a captain—who stood at the helm with an admiration that stirred her. He saw her too. And he did not seek to trap her or tame her. No, he simply watched. Day after day. And she, bewitched, returned to him. Every dawn, she followed."

"They became enamored," I murmured softly.

My gaze sought Rylen's. He was still beside me—but something had shifted. His expression was unreadable, his silence thunderous.

"One could call it enamored," she mused, as though amused by my feeble word. "But she would say it was something deeper. She began to follow him to shore. She lingered, she waited. Days. Weeks. Every time he returned, she offered more of herself. Her love became not an adornment but a tether. Her heart, once her own, no longer pulsed for her—it sang only for him. It belonged to him."

Rylen's body tensed beside me, as if the words struck some old nerve or revelation. His hand cupped my cheek, urgent, trembling. He turned my face to his as though he meant to speak, but no sound came still.

And then—he was gone.

Torn from me by an unseen force, yanked into the deep. The movement was so sudden, so violent, it left only a trail of bubbles and the echo of his name on my lips.

"Rylen!"

I swam forward, heart pounding, limbs heavy, but another hand seized my shoulder. Cold. Commanding.

"Focus, Prince of Gadimore," the voice hissed, honeyed and venom-laced. "Tell me—what do you think becomes of a creature whose existence is bound to a vow, when she gives her heart to another... but that love is not returned?"

The water around me darkened, pulsing with her question. I swallowed, uncertain—tasting salt, silt, and something sharper lodged in my throat. "She died?" I asked.

"In a way," she purred, voice curling around me, "yes. A part of her withered—fractured, beyond the healing of even the sea."

Something unseen brushed my other shoulder—glacial, deliberate. It slid down the length of my arm like a caress with intent, until it curled its fingers around my wrist. It tugged, gently, but with that same steady insistence of the tide. I followed, helplessly tethered, toward the coral structure rising before me like a cathedral twisted by grief. The faint bioluminescence upon the coral pulsed once—brighter—revealing the vague, brooding silhouette of an underwater palace. A crown of ruin etched in stone and shadow.

"Take me to Rylen," I commanded, my voice sharpened ever so slightly.

But she was not finished with her theatre. "The story is not done yet," she said, and the touch vanished, her voice receding like a current into the dark, beckoning me forward.

So I entered.

The archway stood like a wound in the sea, its edge lined with carvings I recognized. Arcanic script—etched deep in the stone—sigils of warding, of silencing. Not just of song, but of any arcane. Born of the sea and not. The hum of it rippled across my skin, a murmur warning.

She was an arcanist.

Within, the chamber yawned wide, a throne room carved from abyssal coral. The black stone gleamed dully in the shifting water, and scattered across the sea bed like forgotten dreams were shards of shattered glass—glinting faintly beneath the algae's green glow.

The silence was unnerving. It was true silence—thick, unnatural. The sea herself was missing from here. The only sound that remained was the low hum of her magic, pulsing steady like a second heartbeat.

I lowered my gaze to the glass below, allowing myself the stillness of focus. "Continue your tale," I said softly. My voice—controlled—cut the silence like a blade drawn slowly from its sheath.

"One day," she began again, "he stopped meeting her at the shore." Her voice, no longer wistful but brittle with buried rage, thickened as she went on. "She had felt it long before—the unraveling of something sacred. A path opened to him, and he took it. He chose a life without her in it."

A pause.

"She mourned. By the sea, how she mourned. She waited—through tides, through seasons. She waited with a hope that rotted slowly from within. He never came. But something else did. *Chaos.*" Her voice grew feverish, electric. "It whispered. It filled her. And it consumed her in ways neither the sea nor the man ever could. But chaos, like men, is a fickle thing. Fleeting. Devouring."

That word—*chaos*—it struck through me.

Rylen had once used that word to describe my arcane.

And suddenly, I understood.

She was a siren.

Not the grotesque imaginings painted by human superstition to demonize merfolk—no. She was *the* siren. The one who haunted the shores of Gadimore, leaving behind broken ships and breathless corpses, hearts hollowed out as if scooped by hand.

A chill prickled across the back of my neck.

And then, in the shards of glass below, her reflection bloomed into clarity—sharp and surreal.

She was beautiful in a way that felt like drowning. Her form glided above me, black hair trailing like ribbons through the water, her tail gleaming with the dusky shimmer of constellations—violet, indigo and black. Her eyes—those terrible, luminous eyes—were the color of bruised plums and moonlit storms. They fastened on me with a hunger that was not lust, but something akin to retribution.

And my body—foolish, trembling—did not know whether to flee or to reach for her.

"Where is Rylen?" I asked, breaking the trance that had laced itself around me.

She smiled. I heard it before I saw it. "Your prince has been near the whole time," she purred.

"Prince?"

"Prince Rylen," she said, each word like a tolling bell. "Prince of the Aserian Sea. Heir to the throne beneath the tides. Prince of the merfolk." She drifted toward the throne, her fingers curling over its back. She gazed at the seat with a reverence that chilled me.

My gaze lowered and settled upon Rylen, his body slumped in the throne. The visage was alarming, he was unmoving, but not lost.

I could feel it, my arcane ebbing, thinning like blood in too much water. The warding sigils etched into this drowned cathedral bled power, and mine faltered beneath it. Each breath grew heavier, slower, more borrowed than earned. I needed to leave. If I lingered, the sea would claim me. But I would not go without him.

"Seems your little prince kept more secrets and lied to you more than you likely perceived," she murmured, circling the throne. "Did he tell you why he walked among humans? Why he sought your kingdom's gilded halls?"

"One cannot lie if I did not wish to know," I said simply.

And it was true. Deep down, I had always known that there was more to him—I knew he was not human but I didn't

understand his motives. When Rylen first arrived at my father's palace, he'd been desperate to see the king. I should have asked why. I should have questioned. But I didn't. I hadn't wanted to know. I wanted to stay in our illusion, our fragile, fleeting bliss. I knew it would end, but I wished to drown in it a while longer.

The siren's eyes glittered like amethyst sunken in the deep. "Your prince is a monster, just like I," she crooned, as though it were a lullaby. "He was to kill your father. And then deliver your heart to me." She watched me. Waiting for a gasp, a tear, a flinch. She found none.

"We are monsters in his eyes," I said. "And I cannot fault a prince for doing what he must for his people."

A pause. Then, a sneer. "How disgustingly noble of you."

She drifted closer to him and my body mirrored hers before my mind could catch up. I moved, protective, instinctual.

"His heart is useless," she said, almost lazily. "Yours had value. But the price was a prince's heart, nonetheless." She pressed a finger to Rylen's chest. He jolted, eyes pressed tightly shut. His back arched; his tail spasmed once, sharp as lightning through dark water.

And then—

Stillness.

The melody that once bound us was gone.

Silenced.

"Rylen!" I cried, my voice cracking in the water, a sound torn from the edge of desperation. I surged forward but she was faster. Her body collided with mine, cold and immovable, the

sharp edge of her grin cutting through what little hope remained.

"I was going to consume your heart, once he'd paid the toll," she whispered, her hands cupping my face with an unsettling softness. "But this pain…" Her thumbs brushed my cheekbones with a lover's gentleness. "The look in your eyes—it's exquisite. It tastes sweeter than chaos. This sorrow, this devastation—it is all I ever wanted to see on a face such as yours."

Her lips curled into something unholy. Her gaze devoured mine. And yes—perhaps my grief betrayed me then. Perhaps, in that moment, she saw everything. But I was not hollow. Not broken. My fingers found the hilt of my sword.

"You and I know what it means to love—not halfway, but completely. To let it consume us, shape us, become the very thread that weaves through who we are." I held her gaze. "But, there is a difference between you and I," I said, my voice low, unshaken. "You let my father go. You let your pain become your crown. I refuse to let go of what is mine."

My blade was slowly drawn.

"You'll never see *your sorrow, your pain* in me," I whispered. "Because this is not mourning. This is fury. This is vengeance."

I drove my blade forward. There was no frenzy, no desperation in the motion. Just certainty. The resistance came first. A brief jarring halt as steel met flesh, and then it gave. Her breath caught. It was not a scream of pain, but a gasp of surprise. As if this outcome had never truly existed to her.

Our bodies remained close. My hand still steady against the hilt, her warmth bleeding into the cold around us as blood seeped from the wound and circled. Her fingers twitched against my cheek, lingering, almost tender. Then they slipped. Her lips parted, something unspoken caught between them and then her gaze finally dimmed.

I let go.

I didn't look back as she sank. My body moved on instinct, already wrapping Rylen in my arms, already swimming, rising, desperate. The weight of him bore down on me, but I held him tighter.

My arcane stirred—weakly at first, then with strength renewed the further I carried us from that cursed abyss. The sea heard me. It answered and we broke the surface to rain and wind and the black velvet of the sky. The moon was gone, shrouded by clouds.

I laid him gently on the sand, the wet earth accepting him like a cradle. Rain fell in ribbons. The tide reached for him—soft, calming—lapping at his tail as if unsure whether to carry him back or bid him farewell.

And I knelt there beside him, my heart a storm. I could not hold it back no longer. The warmth blurred my vision before it spilled, silent, down my cheek. Grief, when true, did not scream—it trembled. And so did I, as my fingertips brushed the cool curve of his face. Still. Too still.

My throat ached with the weight of a cry that would not be given. Instead, I offered what I could, a hum, soft and

breaking. A melody not meant for this world, but for us. Only us. Our song.

This is not the end of our story, I thought, fiercely. *I will not allow it.* My lips found his—featherlight, reverent—as though trying to breathe life into him through stubbornness alone. I whispered against his skin, voice shaking but resolute. "Your heart sings for me. It sings to my tune. It is mine, and it will sing for me forevermore."

I laid beside him then, surrendering to the cold, pressing my head to his chest. Listening. Waiting.

The rain did not fall—it wept. A soft, ceaseless hush that cloaked us in mourning, in solitude. It wrapped itself around us like a shroud, like the hush between the final note and what follows.

My body shivered against his. The warmth that once passed between us like flame had dimmed. My hand, numb but stubborn, traced his skin—down his arm, over his pulse that would not answer. And still, I sang. Quieter now, until even my voice began to silence itself into the hush of grief. But then—there. A flicker. Faint. Fragile.

A beat.

It matched my tune.

My breath caught as I lifted my head, my voice rising again, steadier now, coaxing, pleading. The melody was no longer mine alone. His lips did not move, but he sang back.

I watched as black arcanic script bloomed to life—snaking along his wrist, winding up his arm, and coiling across his chest before vanishing beneath his skin. The beat

grew louder. Color flushed back into his cheeks, warmth returning to his flesh. His lips parted, and then a breath came. Deep, sharp, and beautiful.

"Rylen," I breathed, cupping his cheek.

He did not answer. But his heart did. It beat. Steady. Present. It was as though his soul had been summoned from some distant depth and returned, now pulsing within.

Chapter Ten

I had died.

It was not a tempestuous death. No grand unraveling, no bloodshed. Rather, it came like a forgotten lullaby—soft and still. A slow, fate drawn from within, as though some unseen hand had reached through the hollow of my chest and cradled my heart to silence. I remember the stillness. The absence of breath. The final, fragile beat.

And yet—I awoke.

The water was soft around me, rich with warmth. Above, the cavern shimmered not with stars but with the glow of worms that hung from the stone, their light spilling onto the crystals and creating constellations reborn. I knew this place. The hidden spring beneath the palace of Gadimore.

My body stirred, the long coil of my tail brushing the stillness. My upper half was pressed to something warm—flesh and breath, the steady rhythm of a living heart.

"Titus," I breathed, voice hoarse as the name tumbled from my lips.

He was already looking at me, as if he had not once looked away.

"Where's—"

But I never finished the question. His mouth found mine with an aching urgency. My fingers tangled in his hair, wet and curling like the reeds that cling to shipwrecks. His arms wrapped around me as though they were the only force that could hold me tethered to this world. And perhaps, in that moment, they were.

But something within me shifted.

A tremor in my chest, a faltering note in the rhythm of my heart. I drew back, breath shallow, fingertips grazing the place where my pulse should have been steady. And there—his hand, joining mine.

"I would rather not lie to you," he said, voice low, almost afraid of itself. "Your heart... ceased to beat. But I brought you back."

My breath caught. "How?"

"Please don't be angry with me."

I caught his jaw in my hand, firm, eyes narrowing. "Titus, no. Do not tell me you struck a bargain with her. Morvena's promises are snares. Her tongue is spun with ruin."

He took my wrist gently. "I made no pact," he said, exhaling. "There was no bargain. No plea. I killed her. Though..." His voice caught. "If I'd thought I could trade for your life, I would have. Gods forgive me, I would have."

"You... you killed the seawitch?"

"Yes." The word emerged on a breath. A confession and a release.

The vow was broken. The toll, void. We were no longer bound to her claim.

"How do I live?" I asked, my voice scarcely more than air.

"This is where I may lose your forgiveness." He took my hand, guided it to his chest—over the steady rhythm of his heart. "I tethered our lives, Rylen. Bound my heart to yours, and yours to mine. As long as one beats, so shall the other." His eyes searched mine, raw and aching. "I know it was selfish. I had no right. But you died and something in me broke. I could not—*would not*—let that be the end."

I was silent. There were no ancient rites for this. We had become something new. Something sacred in its defiance.

"I hope," he whispered, "that you can forgive me."

I kissed him. There was nothing left to say, no need for forgiveness, only the meeting of mouths and the tide of something unspeakable rising between us.

"You are not angry?" he murmured, his lips curved faintly against mine.

"How could I be?" I breathed, forehead resting to his. "You saved me. Even knowing what I am. Even after her words. You tethered your life to mine." I drew back, just enough to look into him. "What I cannot understand is... *why*. I am no longer what I was. I am bound in blood and vengeance. I am—"

"A monster?" he finished softly.

I nodded.

He smiled. Not with pity, but with conviction. "I care not what you are. Only that I have you. Because to have you... it is as if I have the kingdom entire, the world, the whole of the sea in my arms. I could never see you as anything less than my own universe."

His gaze held mine, unflinching, and I believed him.

"There is something else I had not told you," I murmured, my voice barely a ripple against the hush of the water between us. "Something from before... this."

My fingers skimmed lightly over my chest, then over his—the phantom tether, our bond.

His gaze held mine, patient, open. Waiting.

"I had already bonded to you," I confessed.

His brows drew together, faintly. "What do you mean?"

"Merfolk mate once, and for life. When it happens, a bond is formed—not unlike the tether you created with your chaos. Though I believe, even before that... the bond had already begun to take root." A warmth crept into my face, a heat so human it almost embarrassed me more.

He smiled softly, that familiar curve of reverence and amusement. Then he pressed a kiss to my brow. "You bonded to me even knowing I couldn't do the same?"

"Yes," I said, quieter now. "I thought I would die. And if I must, I didn't want to pass without claiming what I cherished most. Even if only in my own way."

His laughter was gentle, low, full of some aching fondness. "Who knew you were such a romantic," he said,

brushing a strand of hair from my face. "You know, I always thought you were beautiful—this form especially. Even when we were children." His fingertips traced the glimmering scales that flecked my cheeks. I turned into his touch, but the ache beneath his words lingered.

"Then why didn't you come back?" My voice cracked at the edges despite my efforts. "We promised we'd meet again."

He stilled. Even his breath seemed to pause. "My mother fell ill," he said at last, voice low. "And then... she passed. Even if I had wanted to leave, I was not allowed. When mourning ended, I returned. Every day. For a year, I searched the shore. But I never found you again."

My chest pulled tight, a tide of guilt and softened grief. "I'm sorry. I carried resentment for so long, not knowing. It feels so small now, beside your loss."

"It's not small," he said. "It mattered. And I am sorry I did not recognize you sooner. Deep down I did. But I couldn't place it... Did you know—in this form, you have one hundred twenty-seven freckles? The other only has forty-three. How strange."

I blinked.

"Were you counting them while I slept?"

His smile turned rueful, tender. "When one holds the most beautiful thing the world has ever yielded, one cannot help but learn it—freckle by freckle, breath by breath. To admire is instinct. To remember? That is devotion."

His lips brushed mine, then lingered. A kiss steeped not in heat but in longing, in the gentle terror of being seen and

loved so completely. My breath hitched, and I leaned into him—lost in his taste, the curve of his jaw, the way his hands anchored me like a harbor in the storm.

The song in my chest, the one only he could stir, began again. Not just in the echo of our tether, but in the marrow of who I was. My body yearned, yes, but deeper still—my soul reached. And he wanted me. I could feel it—his arousal unmistakable, pressing against the curve of my tail, the cotton of his trousers no match for the desire that pulsed between us.

"I want to know all of you," I breathed, lips grazing his. "To feel all of you. Every part."

"Then you will," he whispered.

"How much do you know of mer anatomy?" I asked, my voice low and soft.

"Not much," he confessed, gaze dipping with a shyness. Yet his hand, steady and gentle, trailed the length of my tail with a curiosity that stirred the quiet between us into something humming and electric. His touch—tentative, featherlight—skimmed across scales until it slowed over the softer flesh.

"Do you have a..." The rest of the question dissolved into silence, his fingers stilling over the slit nestled within the sleek curve of my tail. I exhaled, breath catching. Gently—so gently—I felt the press. The pad of his finger dipped into those softened scales, and my body answered.

My hand found his shoulder, fingers curling against the warmth of him. "I must warn you," I said, the words thinned by the tremor of anticipation. "My cock is... quite different. It's—"

A moan broke free before I could finish. His finger slid deeper, and with it, my shafts emerged—gliding forth from between the parting scales.

"There's two," he murmured, voice touched by surprise, eyes flicking up to meet mine.

"There's two," I echoed.

His gaze fell again, reverent and slow. "They're... quite a bit larger than a human's," he said, a kind of awe in his words, his fingers grazing one, and I shuddered—utterly undone by the contact.

"We don't have to," I said softly, each syllable a veil of retreat and offering. "If it frightens you. If it's too much."

But he shook his head, firm and full of something tender. "No. I want this. I want *all* of you—no matter the form."

And the way he looked at me then... by the tide, it hollowed me out. In that breathless space, I understood. He wasn't merely giving me his body. He was giving me his trust—wordless, vulnerable, whole.

I watched him peel away the fabric that clung wetly to his skin, each piece falling to the earth with a soft whisper of water and cloth. The stones beneath caught the weight of his offering—bare, deliberate. When at last he turned to face me, there was no shame in his gaze, only quiet eagerness.

"How do we do this?"

"I have never done it before," I confessed. "For us there are no instructions, it is instinct. Will you allow me to follow mine?"

"Yes," Titus whispered. And with that, he drifted backward, his body breaking the water before vanishing beneath the surface.

I followed, my form folding into the water as I reached for him. The moment our bodies met, his magic stirred—the wild hum of his chaos surrounding us, bending the air to cradle his lungs, allowing him to remain below with me.

His lips found mine, warm and seeking. His tongue slid past the seam of my mouth, a welcomed invasion that made my spine shudder. Then his hands lowered, unhesitating, fingers wrapping around both of my shafts with a care that bordered on worship. He aligned them together, his grip firm yet tender as he stroked upward in languid pulls—slow, deliberate, teasing—as if memorizing every inch. My dual lengths pulsed under his touch, slick with their own lubrications.

I groaned into his kiss, my hands slipping to his backside, kneading the firm curve of muscle before spreading him open. My body ached—it ached to claim, to mark, to breed—but I would not take. Not until his body welcomed it.

My hand moved to grasp the head of one of my cocks, pressing firmly against the tip as its natural slickness coated my fingers in a warm, viscous layer. With that digit, I traced the clenched rim of Titus' hole, while my other hand gripped his backside, squeezing and pulling it aside to expose him fully. I circled the puckered entrance, teasing the tight muscle until it quivered under my touch, softening with each deliberate stroke.

I eased one finger inside him, inching forward with deliberate slowness and patience. His lips parted from mine on

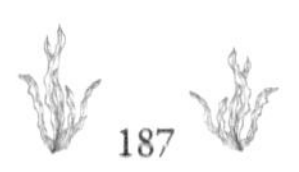

a sharp inhale, a soft moan bubbling between our mouths as his inner walls clamped down around my intrusion—fiercely tight at first, then gradually yielding as I pressed deeper with gentle insistence. His breath hitched against my skin, lips brushing mine once more in the shared heat.

Emboldened by his response, I introduced a second finger, sliding it alongside the first. Titus' body arched subtly in the water, surrendering to the stretch as I worked them in tandem, scissoring to widen the passage and thrusting deeper into the gripping heat.

My mouth skimmed along the taut line of his throat, trailing over his pulse. "Do you believe you're ready?" I murmured, my voice low and thick with raw hunger, yet threaded through with ironclad restraint and patience.

He nodded, and his hands slipped away from my cocks in silent compliance.

I shifted, positioning myself between his thighs. One shaft nestled above the other. I guided the tip of one to his entrance, brushing it tenderly against the soft resistance there.

And then—I entered him slowly.

His body clung to mine, velvet and vice, the heat of him drawing me in. My face buried in the hollow of his neck as I pressed forward, inch by inch, his legs wrapping tightly around my tail. He shuddered in my arms, and I held him, grounded him, matched the rhythm of his breath with my own.

He moved with me, gasping softly, fingers digging into my back as I sank deeper. Every sound he made etched itself into me like a song.

And still—I wanted more. *Needed* more.

He felt it, our souls in sync. His hand slipped behind him, fingers curling around the second shaft, stroking the one I had denied. "Rylen," he said, voice ragged and full of promise, "I can take it."

The tether of my restraint snapped.

I seized him gently—though my hunger was anything but—and guided us to the bottom of the spring. The soft thud of his body meeting the bed stirred a bloom of sand around us. I pinned him there, my fingers splayed against his chest. I withdrew, aligned both swollen tips to his already gaping hole, and pushed forward.

Slowly. Devoutly.

The tantalizing squeeze of his body against my cocks coaxed more slickness. It was nature's own offering—an aching, liquid ease that made every movement between us more fluid, more unbearably sweet.

He arched, back bowing. His fingers clawed at the riverbed, his moan soft and shattering.

I pressed deeper, inch by careful inch, savoring the way his body yielded around me—tight and trembling. Every heartbeat, every shuddered breath was a hymn offered to the sacred rhythm between us.

The water around us rippled with our movements. His thighs gripped me tighter, hips urging and pleading. And answered without words. My pace quickened, hips driving deeper with each thrust, chasing the sharp, golden edge of pleasure that thrummed just out of reach—the release we both

craved, desperate and pure, a need that eclipsed thought and reason alike.

He moaned—a broken, beautiful sound—and the world inside me shattered and rebuilt itself around him. "Ry—" he gasped, and the sound was music. His release spilled into the water, mingling with the spring's shimmer. But I hadn't finished.

I drove into him with a hunger, my shafts throbbing, aching for that final undoing for myself. The world had narrowed to this—his body clutching at mine, the molten pull of pleasure drawing tighter, tighter, until I could no longer tell where he ended and I began.

The friction turned sinuous, each motion made smoother, deeper, more devastatingly pleasing. My senses drowned in him. Each thrust became a vow unspoken, a confession etched into flesh rather than words.

And then—

I broke.

Ecstasy, pure and searing, flooded through me. My body seized, my tail flicking violently through the water, stirring up clouds of sand as a ragged cry tore from my throat—raw, wordless, a sound born from the primal, most desperate part of me.

I spilled into him with abandon, filling his stretched, trembling hole until my seed could no longer be contained. It seeped out around me, thick and warm, ribbons of it carried by the currents that our bodies had churned into a frenzy.

Even as the tremors wracked my body, even as the last shudders of my climax faded into the water around us, I stayed, buried deep within him, unwilling—unable—to part from the place where he had so freely accepted all that I was. The urge remained—to fill him, to claim him, to offer all of myself and take all of him in turn.

But I resisted.

I began to withdraw, only for his legs to lock around me. His arms pulled me down. And then, before I could protest, his chaos surged. The water twisted with his command, turning on itself like a whirlpool, and suddenly, I was beneath him, my back pressed against the sediment.

He straddled me, eyes glazed with want, heavy with something deeper than lust. Possession. Bond.

He lowered himself onto me again, hips rolling with divine precision. My fingers clutched his thighs, claws grazing flesh as he moved—using me, riding me, as though he'd been made for this.

This—

This was how it felt to mate with one's bonded.

A feeling so intoxicating, so ruinous in its tenderness, it seemed almost too vast for the fragile shell of our mortal bodies to contain.

Our melody flooded the space around us. The water itself pulsed with it, shivering with every beat of our hearts, every trembling gasp, as if the spring had been stirred awake by the force of our union.

I rose to meet him, fingers threading into the flowing silks of his hair. I pulled him to me, unable to bear even a breath's distance between us, and crushed our mouths together. His lips parted willingly against mine—soft, yielding, tasting of salt and need and the wild sweetness that was him.

He was the finest thing I had ever tasted—whether above the waves or beneath them—and he was all mine. And I was his.

Wholly.

Fully.

In every aching, starved corner of my being. There would be no separating us. No tide strong enough, no kingdom vast enough to tear me from him. We were bound.

Irrevocably, gloriously bound.

My arms draped over the stone lip of the spring, the roughness of ancient rock pressing against my forearms. Beneath me, my tail stirred the water in languid, sighing currents, a restless echo of my thoughts. I watched as Titus pulled himself from the pool, water sliding from his skin in gleaming rivulets.

The air, once crisp and cool, shifted strangely—warm now, heavy, as it bent to his chaos.

"A trick I learned in younger days," he said, reaching for the sodden pile of his garments. His voice carried that

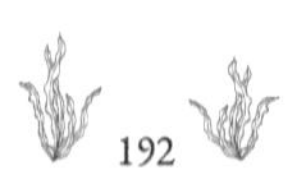

half-laugh of old mischiefs fondly remembered. "I was ever reckless—riding out against better judgement, no matter how the clouds warned me. I would return to the palace, boasting I had outrun the rain itself… though the muck on my boots and the damp in my hair gave me away."

I watched, bemused, as the water fled his clothes at a mere brush of his hand, leaving the fabric dry and obedient.

"You have a rather stubborn spirit, it seems," I said, my voice purring low in the misted cavern. "Tell me, prince—where does your kingdom believe you have spirited yourself away to?"

He stilled for a beat, slipping an arm into his linen shirt with careful grace, but the silence between us sharpened.

It had been a long night—one stitched with sorrow and softened by love—but even here, in this stolen haven, we could not hold the world at bay forever.

"It is no rare thing for me to disappear," he said at length. "I offered no explanation."

A quiet hum escaped me, not unkind. "Surely they do not believe their crowned grand admiral has abandoned his banquet merely for duty's sake. You ran not to the fleet, nor to royal expectations. You ran from the woman they promised you… to chase a man instead."

I let the words linger, half a question dressed as a statement, watching his face for the truth of it. "Or do they believe you have given chase to the mer, cloaked in human guise, who killed your men?"

His brow furrowed as he turned to me fully, the shirt falling forgotten at his side. "You killed my men?"

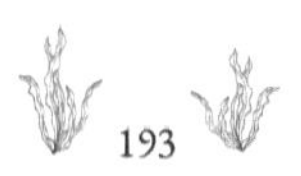

The words were stripped bare, hard to read, neither accusation nor absolution.

I met his gaze, the old guilt tightening around my throat. "Is that not what your captain came to tell you?"

"Captain LeVesque returned to report," Titus said, stepping closer. "But there was no mention of merfolk. Rylen—" He crouched, bringing his face level with mine, the worm's glow catching in his eyes like stars. "The blood you think stains your hands—it is not mine to hold against you. You slew men, yes. But not my men."

"I do not understand."

"LeVesque's report spoke of pirates," he said. "It was they who butchered my fleet. You merely avenged them. Captain LeVesque survived, found by another Gadimore ship by the grace of the sea itself."

I stared at him, unblinking, the words heavy and strange in my mind.

"Pirates?" I repeated, my voice a whisper.

He nodded. "Pirates. Rogues who honor no crown. Men who plunder and destroy, heedless of who they harm. It is against such men my fleet sail to protect human and mer alike."

And in that instant, the fragile edifice of certainty I had built within me cracked and crumbled. Morvena had lied. She had twisted my anger, fed it falsehoods until I was a monster wielded on her behalf.

I began to slip lower into the water, the urge to vanish, to drown in my own foolishness, pulling at me—but his hand

caught my wrist, strong and sure, drawing me back to the surface.

"Stop," he murmured, and the word held such tender command that I stilled at once. "This is a mercy, Rylen," he said, his voice a low hymn. "You are innocent of the crimes you feared. And it paves the way for what I must ask of you."

I could only gaze at him, my heart caught fast between my ribs.

"I told you before—I want you. All of you. And I would sooner cast aside crown and country than hide what I feel. If they would have me, they must have me as I am—a man who will marry another man."

My heart trembled, the tide of him breaking over me. "And if they will not?" I whispered.

"Then let them lose me," he said simply, as though it were the easiest conclusion in the world. "A kingdom should not fall from the absence of one man. I will follow you, wherever your path winds—whether they bless us or curse us. I will always follow my heart."

His hand rose to my face, the pad of his thumb tracing the curve of my cheekbone with aching fondness. "You," he said, his voice scarcely more than breath, "are my heart."

I closed my fingers over his, guiding his palm to my lips and pressing a kiss there. "Even your words drip with princely virtue," I teased, my voice roughened by emotion. "It is insufferable."

"And let us not forget," he said, a smile tugging at the corner of his mouth, "that you are no less royal. Rylen, Prince of the Aserian Sea."

The name curled between us like a benediction.

He laughed softly, the sound low and rich. "It is only fitting, is it not? That the prince who guards the shores should marry the prince who rules the tides? A match both political and poetic, if we must speak diplomatically."

I found myself laughing too, the sound bright and disbelieving.

"I wish to be where you are as well," I murmured. "But I would never seek to tear you from your kingdom—if they will have you. There is... a problem here." My voice thinned, the waters sighing around me as my tail sliced across the surface, casting a soft spray before it disappeared beneath once more. "A problem that would keep you from the land, if you chose to remain with me."

He stepped away. "I had thought of that, actually." His tone bore the familiar lilt of mischief, yet something steadier thrummed beneath it. "I had time to think, as I waited for you to wake."

He crouched by his discarded coat, fingers moving deftly through the fabric until he unearthed something small. "There was a talisman you cast aside, before you returned to the sea. I could feel the arcane humming through it. I kept it. It sang of transmutation—faintly, but enough for me to recognize and learn. I've little experience with such magic, but then again..."

He shot me a smug smile over his shoulder. "I never thought I could bring someone back from death, either."

A wry laugh slipped from him as he rose. "I believe I managed to mimic her spell."

"You *believe*?" I arched a brow, skepticism and a traitorous flicker of hope coiling through my chest.

"I had no chance to test it." He returned to me, his hands careful. "Hold out your hand."

I obeyed, palm up, water dripping in lazy rivulets down my arm. He dropped something into my grasp.

"Is this..?"

My breath caught, my gaze widening as I lifted the shell from my palm. It was small, cool as wintertide against my skin, and thrummed faintly with the pulse of magic—chaotic, familiar, his. I traced its delicate ridges with reverent fingers, as though it might vanish under too rough a touch.

"The same one," Titus said, his voice edged with a boyish chuckle, a tilt to his smile that crinkled the corners of his eyes.

"You kept it?" I whispered, my heart stirring like a tide under a sudden wind.

"Of course I did. A friend gave it to me. Why would I rid myself of it?" He pressed his lips to my brow with a tenderness that ached.

"Friend?" I echoed, my fingers curling into the back of his neck, pulling him nearer.

He chuckled low, his breath warm against my mouth. "Well, I did not yet know you were my lover."

I kissed him, slow and tenderly, and when he pulled back, the world seemed quieter somehow, steadier.

"So," he said, another kiss brushed fleetingly to my lips before he straightened, "if I have done this correctly—I am Gadimore's greatest arcanist, after all—so surely I had."

"Surely," I teased, feigning grave solemnity.

His gaze narrowed, the threat of a grin tugging at his mouth. "All you must do is hold the shell and attune yourself to the song of the world you wish to be part of—land or sea. Your body will answer."

I turned the shell between my fingers. "Would it work on you?"

He hesitated, then laughed. "I—suppose it would, yes. Why? Do you wish to see me with a tail?"

I allowed a small smile to bloom. "It would be a fine thing... to have you swim the ocean with me, just as I will walk the earth with you."

"I would gladly follow you into the deep, Rylen," he said, and there was such fierce, unvarnished sweetness in him that made my heart ache. "If that is where you wish me to be. Then I will be."

Chapter Eleven

"I had sent men to find you," King Evren's voice cut through the heavy door of the study, low and stern, though the threads of worry beneath it were not so easily hidden. "All they found was Brisa. The worst was assumed, Titus. You cannot simply vanish. Not when you bear the weight of this kingdom. Not when alliances hang so precariously in the balance."

Beside me, Elisienne leaned in close, her whisper a soft breath against the hush of the corridor.

"Perhaps you would be more comfortable waiting elsewhere?"

I shook my head, lifting my chin with quiet resolve. "No. Titus bade me wait here."

"As you wish," she murmured, dipping into a graceful curtsy before her footsteps faded down the marble hall, leaving me alone.

Within the study, the king's voice pressed harder.

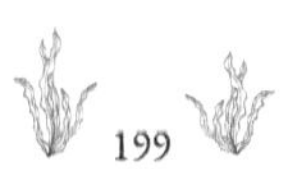

"Where were you?" His words, though measured, carried the cold steel of command. "I will not ask again."

My fingers slipped into my pocket, seeking the shell hidden there—the little relic of chaos and devotion. I traced its curve absently, grounding myself in its familiar song.

Titus, ever so confident with his men, his nobles, even the faceless court, now hesitated in front of his father. "I was..." A pause, like the faltering of breath. "It is difficult to explain without... context. I—"

It was painful to hear him falter beneath the weight of expectation, the shadow of disappointment from not only his people but from his father if he continued to speak. I did not let him struggle further. Not alone at least. With a gentle push, I opened the doors. The guards tensed, hands going to their hilts, but a single sharp dismissive wave from Titus stilled them.

Lowering my head with the proper measure of human courtly grace, I stepped forward. "I beg your pardon, Your Majesty, for the interruption."

King Evren's gaze snapped to me, heavy with scrutiny. "And who might this be?"

"This is—" Titus began, but I cut in, my voice steady.

"Rylen," I said, meeting the king's eyes unflinchingly. "Prince of Aserian."

I could feel Evren weighing me, piece by piece.

"I was told of a visitor by that name," he said slowly. "But none spoke of royal blood... You say Aserian?" His brow arched with pointed skepticism. "As in the sea?"

"The very same," I answered, inclining my head with all the deference his station demanded—but not an inch more. "And if it pleases Your Majesty, I would request privacy for this conversation. Matters such as these deserve no audience."

"I fail to see the point of this intrusion," his gaze shifted to Titus. "Is this not the man who has lost his mind?"

"Please, just hear him out," Titus said, his voice low with weariness as he released a slow, measured sigh.

A beat of silence passed, measured and thick.

"Very well," the king said at last, a flick of his wrist sending the guards retreating. The heavy doors thudded shut behind them, leaving the three of us alone.

Only then did I truly lift my gaze to take in the private sanctuary of the king. A solemn chamber, paneled in dark, gleaming woods. Maps were unfurled across a vast oak table. Shelves lined the walls, crammed with ledgers and brittle scrolls bound in faded leather. It smelled of parchment, iron, and the sea. This was the works of a man who ruled not just from a throne but from the prow of a ship.

And in the heart of it stood Titus, caught between two worlds, with me.

"You say you are from the Aserian Sea?" King Evren's voice cut through the stillness once more, heavier now, weighted with things unspoken.

"Yes," I replied, crossing the chamber in slow, measured steps. My fingers skimmed across the sprawling map that lay atop the great oak table, tracing the delicate etchings until they

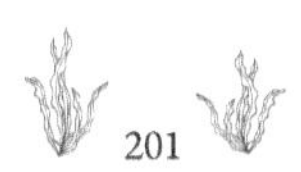

hovered over the outline of Gadimore. I lifted my gaze to meet his.

"I would say our kingdoms have never formally met before, but that would be a lie. I understand you were once acquainted with my cousin—Lady Morvena, as you would call her in your courtly tongue."

At the name, a flicker of recognition—and something more pained crossed Evren's features. "Morvena," he echoed, voice roughened with memory. "You are merfolk."

"I am," I answered simply, letting the truth sit heavy in the air. "And I have come to make an offer for your son's hand in marriage."

The weight of the room shifted, invisible but palpable. Evren's eyes snapped to Titus, who looked momentarily stunned by the boldness of my declaration. Yet as our eyes met, I saw the corners of his mouth soften, the tension in his shoulders melt away.

"My son is already promised," Evren said stiffly. "To Princess Seraphina of Balthvidae. And even if he were not, he cannot be promised to... another man."

"Where I come from," I said, my voice gentle but unwavering, "it matters not the gender of one's beloved—only that love itself is true."

Evren turned to Titus, his voice strained with something between disbelief and fear. "Titus. Are you in love with this man—merman?"

Titus did not falter. "I am," he said, stepping boldly away from his father's side to stand beside me. His hand found

mine, and we entwined our fingers without shame, without hesitation.

The king's face crumpled with a sorrow that carved deeper than anger. His hand rose to rub wearily at his brow. "You know I wish only for your happiness. But I cannot allow this. You are bound to Seraphina. Breaking that vow would jeopardize a trade alliance... it would jeopardize our legacy."

"*Legacy*," Titus echoed, a rough laugh escaping him, low and bitter. "Is legacy only the sons I might produce? What of the legacy of change? Of a kingdom that dares to be more than what it was yesterday? Prosperity I could bring—not just to Gadimore, but to all of Lopharius. And with Rylen at my side... with Aserian beside us... imagine what more we could be."

"It is forbidden," Evren said, though he sounded less like a king now and more like a man weighed down by ancient chains he was too afraid to cast off.

Titus stepped forward, the defiance in him tempered only by the sorrow in his eyes. "What happened to the man who once fought for change? You were the one who made the sea safer for merfolk—for Morvena, weren't you?"

Evren's throat bobbed, his silence speaking louder than words.

"Then do this for me." Titus' gaze flickered to me, soft but resolute. "This... is forbidden only if you say it is."

"They could turn on us," Evren said, as though saying it aloud would make the fear easier to bear.

"For what? For love? For choosing a partner who strengthens me rather than diminishes me? Tell me, Father,

how does who I share my bed with dictate how I lead? How does it make me less fit to rule? Give me one true reason—only one—and I will say no more."

Silence swallowed the room whole.

Evren opened his mouth, but no words came.

"You chose duty once, and I am grateful you found love with my mother," Titus continued, quieter now. "But I will always choose my heart. That is my duty. That is my honor. If you cannot allow it, I will leave," he swallowed, "and you will have nothing."

The words hung in the air, heavy as a final judgment.

"Or," I spoke, letting my voice slip in, steady and sure, "you can take Gadimore toward a new era of progression. Of expansion. As I understand it, you humans have a long tradition of using your offspring as tokens in alliances. I offer myself on behalf of Aserian. I offer you more than a name. I offer the deep."

My gaze met Evren's without wavering.

"As Titus said, with Aserian at Gadimore's side, with our union, your influence will reach beyond Lopharius. Trade routes will cross the Aserian Sea under your banners. Pirates, raiders—those who prey on the vulnerable—you will have our aid in driving them back. There are treasures lost to the deep and treasures yet to be unearthed. All of it yours, with the agreement that my people are the ones to retrieve what the sea has hidden."

At my words, Titus turned toward me, surprise flaring in his eyes—a mixture of awe and something softer, deeper.

Evren said nothing. Instead, he drifted toward the map, his fingers hovering over Gadimore, tracing unseen lines toward distant waters, weighing Balthvidae's promises against the riches of the unknown.

"If I were a woman," I said, "would you have accepted my offer without hesitation?" I stepped forward, my voice sharpening. "If the answer is yes... then I believe we have nothing further to discuss."

"You are right," Evren said at last, voice measured. "If this offer had come from an emissary speaking for a princess, I would not have second-guessed it. This is a far better alliance than what Balthvidae has placed on the table—expansion of trade on the continent into their kingdom alone. With you, Gadimore can look beyond Lopharius."

He turned his gaze fully to me.

"And... I would be a hypocrite to deny this union because you are not human." His mouth pressed into a thin line. "But—" His eyes shifted to Titus, something heavy shadowing his features. "I am unsure of my ability to protect my son from the backlash of the more... pressing matter."

"I don't need protection," Titus said softly, yet firmly. "I only seek your acceptance. Your blessing. Regardless, I will marry Rylen. The choice is yours, father: whether you wish to still have me by your side—or not."

"I will always have you," Evren murmured, the weight of those words sinking deep. "You are my son."

Titus stepped forward without hesitation, gathering his father into his arms. For a heartbeat, Evren remained still,

as if struggling against a tide unseen. But then a low sigh escaped him, and his arms closed around Titus in return. His eyes shut tightly, as though sealing away everything but this—this quiet, fragile moment between a father and the son he had nearly lost.

The embrace was not one of kings and heirs, but one with the raw tenderness of a father and son. When he finally pulled away, he placed his hands on Titus' shoulders, holding him at arm's length. "If this is what you desire," he said, the words rough but sure, "then I will make it so." His gaze lifted to meet mine, steady and unblinking. "I require a meeting with Aserian's current crown. Will you be able to arrange that?"

"Of course, Your Highness," I answered, relief washing through me so strongly my knees nearly gave out.

But no sooner had the weight lifted than a new, colder realization set in. I had been gone from Aserian for days—vanished once, and then again. And this second time... rumors surely would have spread. Whispers that a human had slain the seawitch and stolen the sea's lost prince. And somewhere beyond these stone walls, the tide of consequence was already rising.

"You told them we fornicated?" Titus' eyes widened, his gaze darting to the shoreline where my mother and father stood, the

sea rising beneath, carrying them level to where King Evren waited atop the stone dock.

"I had to," I said with a chuckle, my hands gently finding his wrists, pulling his hands away from his face to reveal his handsome but very red expression. "It was the only way they would understand how serious this is."

"Does this mean they hate me?" he muttered.

"You deliberately disobeyed us," my mother's voice rang in my mind, sharp and clear. "None of this would have happened had you stayed away from the surface. No blood would have been spilled, no merfolk would have been captured if we had simply remained where we belong."

My gaze drifted past them, to the expanse of the palace. Its walls were carved from stone and coral, stretching high above into the shadowed water. Glowing algae clung to the ceiling, weaving across it like the stars themselves had fallen and tangled with a rainbow. Fish and merfolk alike swam through grand openings framed with spiraling shells and luminous anemones, the current carrying them through the living heart of the sea.

This was safety, yes. This was beauty beyond compare. But it was unjust that we should remain hidden beneath, when so much of the sea and the world beyond awaited us.

My father rose from his throne of pearl and white stone, the heavy silence he had kept since my return finally breaking.

"You sought revenge against the humans, and look what it has cost us," he said, voice low and strained.

"Morvena—your cousin, *my niece*—is lost. And you..." His grip tightened on the trident he held, the muscles in his arm tensing as he fought for control. "You have changed. I can feel it in the current around you. I can see it in your eyes. The surface has touched you."

His knuckles whitened around the trident, the anger and grief barely contained.

"And now you wish to leave us again. For a human."

"But father, I..." My voice caught, but I forced the words out. "I love him."

"A mer cannot be with a human. They are monsters. They are the reason we hide in the deep," he bit out.

"Not all are monsters," I said quietly, my gaze lowering. "Just as not all of us are like Morvena."

I let the words settle between us.

"It was a mer who gave me the means to walk the surface. It was a mer who manipulated me. A mer who killed me." My fingers brushed over my chest to the phantom ache stirring beneath the skin. "But it was a human who found me. A human who sheltered me when I was lost. A human who took care of me in a place I didn't belong. A human who showed me love. And it was a human who saved my life."

I lifted my gaze back to my father's. "I would not be breathing if not for him."

"That still does not change the truth that you are of the sea, and he is not," my mother said at last, a soft sigh threading through her words. Her hands came to rest upon my father's

shoulders, and I watched as the tension slowly drained from him, the rigid set of his spine easing under her touch.

"Our people are not so different. There are many among us—mer and human alike—who wish for nothing more than to live their lives in peace, to do good. I believe we can bridge the gap between our worlds. We can learn from each other, help one another evolve. Imagine how wondrous it would be to traverse the waters fully. To bask beneath the sun, to dance upon the surface of the sea as freely as we do below."

"You wish to form an alliance with the humans?" my mother asked, her tone soft, though a shadow of worry creased her brow.

"Yes," I said simply. "I have bonded with the human prince of Gadimore."

"Bonded?" my father's voice rose, rough as a breaking wave. The furious flush in his face deepened the contrast of the gray and white streaks threading through his dark hair and beard.

"*No, no...*" I murmured to Titus, my hand finding his as I pushed back the rush of memories. His boots shifted uncertainly against the sands.

"Swear to me then,"

"Maybe a little," I said instead, smiling up at him, unable to help the joy that lit my features, "but you are you. Everyone will love you, just as I do. It may take time, but they will come to see you as I see you."

My fingers brushed along the sharp angle of his jaw before cupping his face. I rose to kiss him with all the certainty and softness I could.

Titus leaned his forehead against mine, his hand cradling my cheek, grounding me. "So they are... alright with this? You marrying a human prince?" he whispered.

"They have no choice," I whispered back, brushing my thumb over his skin. "We are bonded. Were we to be torn apart, they would risk me falling as Morvena did." I pressed another kiss to his lips, lingering in the moment until a voice carried across the sands—my mother's, calling to me.

We turned to find all three of them staring at us. It was an odd sight: my mother, my father, and King Evren, gathered beneath the bleeding hues of the setting sun. Merfolk and human. Rulers of two worlds, bound together by a love neither of them had expected us to find.

When I first set upon my quest for vengeance, heart brimming with grief and rage, I had never thought it would lead me here. To him. To this.

"Come. I think it's time for you to meet the King and Queen of Aserian," I whispered, before I slipped my fingers through his and led him forward.

"Oh," I added with a mischievous glint, "I forgot to warn you. My mother has insisted that heirs be part of the alliance."

"Heirs?" His steps slowed.

"If you take on the form of a mer, you should be able to mate with me and do so."

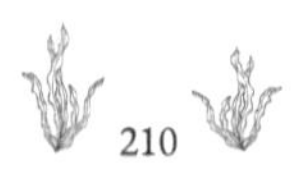

His cheeks reddened so deeply it nearly matched the sky. "You are saying... we could have children together?" he asked, voice almost boyish with hope.

"Yes." I laughed softly, warmth blooming in my chest. "Would that be something you would want?"

He stopped entirely then, turning me to face him fully, his hands cradling mine between them. "With you?" he said, the words trembling with feeling. "Yes. More than anything. I had not thought about it, but now that you say it—yes. I want a piece of both of us in this world." He hesitated. "But... what if it doesn't work? I'm not truly of the sea."

I leaned in close, tilting my head playfully. "Then you will simply have to breed me until it does."

Titus choked, his ears burning. "I—I... yes, of course, I will... breed you."

I couldn't help but laugh, the sound bubbling up between us.

"Do not laugh at me," he said, though he chuckled too, bashful and endearing. "I do not understand how any of this works."

"So endearing, my prince," I whispered, pressing a kiss to his flushed cheek.

He smiled at me then, loving and soft, and in that moment as we stood where the tides meet and the future unfurled ahead of us, I knew there was nowhere else in all the worlds I would rather be.

Epilogue

"Nerina! Nerídes! Don't run, please," I called out as the patter of their feet echoed along the wooden deck, their laughter trailing behind them as they disappeared up the quarterdeck. My heart tightened in my chest, watching them vanish from sight.

"You worry too much," Titus murmured, his breath warm against my neck as he wrapped his arms around me, drawing my back flush against his chest.

"What if they fall and break a bone? Humans are such fragile beings," I sighed, though I leaned into him, finding comfort in his embrace.

He leaned back slightly, raising his voice above the sigh of the sea. "Rina and Édes, listen to your father or I will hoist the anchor and we'll—" The unmistakable splash of bodies hitting water interrupted him—once, then twice. He sighed, defeated. "Well, there they go."

A soft laugh escaped me. "Part of me is jealous of them. Grateful, too—that they can shift between forms so easily. No pain, no hardship. Just... second nature." My fingers wove into the hair at the back of his head, idly playing with the strands. "Still, sometimes I wish the change took longer. Maybe then they wouldn't always swim off the moment trouble catches up to them. I'd wager they're already halfway to my mother and father to complain that I scold them too much."

Titus chuckled lowly. "If only you were born a cichlid. You could keep the twins safe in your mouth and never have to worry."

I elbowed him gently.

"Ow," he feigned dramatically. "That's not how you should treat your husband. Especially when the twins are away with the grandparents." His lips brushed my skin, a slow, deliberate trail that sent a shiver through me. "We could use this time for..."

He didn't need to finish.

The way his body pressed against mine—hot, insistent—the way his hand drifted down my stomach, fingers teasing the edge of my trousers... it was enough. A silent promise burning between us. But just as the moment bloomed, it was snuffed out just as swiftly.

"Fathers!" Nerídes shouted from the waters below, excitement bright in his voice.

We stepped to the railing, leaning over the sun-warmed wood to peer below. There, cutting through the water like twin streaks of light, Nerina and Édes swam lazily at the surface,

their laughter bubbling up like music. They were the perfect tapestry of us—woven from my soul and his. A beautiful reflection of all that we were: adventurous, curious, and stubborn beyond reason.

"We found a fish that looks exactly like Grandfather Evren!" Nerina called up, unable to stifle her giggles. "Can we keep him? Please?"

"No, you cannot keep the fish!" Titus called back. "He belongs to the sea." He paused, brow furrowing. "Wait—how much does he look like him? Because depending on the resemblance, I might reconsider."

"Leave the poor fish alone," I added, fighting a smile.

"But he wants to live with us!" Édes chimed in, his pout carrying even from the water.

"You live on land and sea—you may visit him whenever you wish, but he stays where he belongs," I said, a sternness in my voice that only half-masked the amusement.

The twins sighed in unison before submerging once more, vanishing beneath the shimmering surface.

Titus turned back to me with a wicked smile, cornering me gently against the rail. His hands framed me, palms braced on either side, trapping me there with all the warmth of him. "Now... where were we?" he murmured.

My hands slid up his shoulders, slow and teasing, as I leaned in and brushed my lips against his. "I believe you were about to tell me how a good husband ought to treat his beloved," I whispered, voice low and playful.

"See? Look at him!" Nerina's voice rang out once more, triumphant.

Titus' head fell forward in mock defeat.

I glanced back over the railing and sure enough—a plump, wide-eyed fish with an uncanny resemblance to King Evren floated near the surface.

I couldn't help the laugh that broke free. "He does look like him," I admitted, nudging Titus. "But no, you still cannot keep him."

I pressed a kiss to his cheek before lightly pushing him back. "Another time, my love."

"Another time," he echoed, smiling as he joined me in resting his forearms on the railing, side by side.

"It still feels surreal that this is us now," Titus murmured, his voice a soft hum against the salt-kissed air.

"It's been eight years, and you still can't believe it?" I teased gently.

"It's hard to believe when one's life feels like a dream," he said, smiling—that same soft, adoring smile he had worn since the first day. A look that had never once faded, no matter the trials we had weathered.

"The difference between this and a dream," I whispered, leaning into him, my head resting lightly against his shoulder, "is that dreams end. They fade from memory, lost to time."

I closed my eyes for a breath, feeling his warmth against me.

"Our story never ends. A chapter may close, but another will always begin. It'll always be you and me. Forever."

"Always and forever," he echoed, his voice like a vow whispered into the sea breeze. "Swear to it?"

"A mer's promise," I said, pressing a kiss to his cheek. "Always and forever."

Together, we stood at the railing, watching the endless stretch of water shimmer beneath the setting sun. Our children's laughter floated up from below, their luminous forms darting just beneath the surface, diving deep before breaching the waves in a joyous, endless dance.

We were not tethered to one world or the other. The only anchor that held us steady was love—ours, and the beautiful lives we had brought into existence.

NOTE FROM THE AUTHOR

Thank you so much for taking the time to read my story! I hope you found something meaningful in this achillean reimagining of *The Little Mermaid*—and that the love shared between Rylen and Titus brought you as much comfort and hope as it did for me while writing it.

I'd be truly grateful if you could take a moment to leave an honest review and rating on Goodreads, Amazon, or any other platform you prefer. Your feedback makes a world of difference for small authors like me. If you'd like to learn more about me, explore my other works, or check out upcoming projects, please visit https://elijahher.com.

Thank you again for your support!

OTHER WORKS BY ELIJAH HER

"Binds of the Forsaken"

"Her Majesty's Captain"

"Ascendance of the Forgotten Prince"

and a few web-novels that are only available on Tapas.

CHARACTERS OF WtTM

Rylen (He/Him)

Age: 20

Sexual Orientation: Bisexual

Species: Merfolk

Personality Type & Sign: INFJ, Scorpio

Physical Descriptions: Blue Eyes, Black-Blue Hair, 5'11"

Favorites: Sea Lavender, White Lotus, Swimming, Twilight, Shell Hunting, Honey and other sweets

Titus Beaumir (He/Him)

Age: 19

Sexual Orientation: Gay

Species: Human

Personality Type & Sign: ISFJ, Leo

Physical Descriptions: Green Eyes, Brown Hair, 6'0"

Favorites: Horseback Riding, Sailing, Piano, Spiced Red Wine, Savory Foods